"Oh, Tori. You deserve so much more.

"You don't need to settle for anything less than it all." Nate took her hand, raised it to his lips and placed a kiss against her fingers. She felt the jolt all the way up her arm, saw the desire in his eyes. "I'm going to say good night now, before I get into any more trouble," he whispered. With a squeeze of her hand, he released her, then walked down the stairs.

Tori fought to keep from calling him back and asking him to stay with her, to ease her loneliness. She closed her eyes and relived Nate's kiss, the gentleness of his touch against her skin. What would it be like if she hadn't sent the good-looking sheriff home tonight? As much as she tried to deny it, she wanted Nate Hunter. What would it be like to make love with him? She blew out a long breath.

That was a fantasy she couldn't let come true.

Dear Reader,

What are your favorite memories of summer? Even though I spend my days reading manuscripts, I love nothing better than basking in the sun's warm glow as I sit immersed in a great book. If you share this pleasure with me, rest assured that I can make packing your beach bag *really* easy this month!

Certainly, you'll want to make room in your bag for Patricia Thayer's *A Taste of Paradise* (SR #1770), part of the author's new LOVE AT THE GOODTIME CAFÉ miniseries. Thayer proves that romance is the order of the day when a sexy sheriff determined to buy back his family's ranch crosses paths with a beautiful blond socialite who is on the run from an arranged marriage. Watch the sparks fly in *Rich, Rugged...Royal* by Cynthia Rutledge (SR #1771) in which an ordinary woman discovers that the man whom she had a one-night affair with is not only her roommate but also a royal! International bestselling author Lilian Darcy offers an emotional tale about an estranged couple who are reunited when the hero is named bachelor of the year, in *The Millionaire's Cinderella Wife* (SR #1772). Finally, I'm delighted to introduce you to debut author Karen Potter whose *Daddy in Waiting* (SR #1773) shows how a mix-up at a fertility clinic leads to happily ever after.

And be sure to leave some room in your bag next month when Judy Duarte kicks off a summer-themed continuity set at a county fair!

Happy reading,

Ann Leslie Tuttle
Associate Senior Editor

Please address questions and book requests to:
Silhouette Reader Service
U.S.: 3010 Walden Ave., P.O. Box 1325, Buffalo, NY 14269
Canadian: P.O. Box 609, Fort Erie, Ont. L2A 5X3

PATRICIA THAYER

A Taste of Paradise

SILHOUETTE **Romance**®

Published by Silhouette Books

America's Publisher of Contemporary Romance

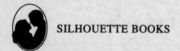 SILHOUETTE BOOKS

ISBN 0-373-19770-5

A TASTE OF PARADISE

Visit Silhouette Books at www.eHarlequin.com

Printed in U.S.A.

PATRICIA THAYER

has been writing for sixteen years and has published nineteen books with Silhouette. Her books have been nominated for the National Readers' Choice Award, Virginia Romance Writers of America's Holt Medallion, Orange Rose Contest and a prestigious RITA® Award. In 1997, *Nothing Short of a Miracle* won the *Romantic Times* Reviewers' Choice Award for Best Special Edition.

Thanks to the understanding men in her life—her husband of thirty-two years, Steve, and her three grown sons and two grandsons—Pat has been able to fulfill her dream of writing romance. Another dream is to own a cabin in Colorado, where she can spend her days writing and her evenings with her favorite hero, Steve. She loves to hear from readers. You can write to her at P.O. Box 6251, Anaheim, CA 92816-0251, or check her Web site at www.patriciathayer.com for upcoming books.

Prologue

"A merger for a marriage." Jed Foster's voice sounded confident, almost smug. "I have to admit you really came through, J.C."

Tori's breath stopped as she removed her hand from the doorknob and forced herself to listen to the conversation between her father and the man she would marry in the morning.

"I told you not to worry," J.C. assured his future son-in-law. "The wedding is in less than eighteen hours and by the end of the month, your company will be part of Sherco. Tori, being married, finally gets her control of her grandfather's stock. Between the two of us, we'll have the majority shares. Now it will be up to you to convince Tori how to vote her shares."

"That shouldn't be too hard. I've been able to persuade her to see things my way for months."

Tori felt sick, hearing the satisfaction in her fiancé's voice. Her grandfather's will had been ironclad. She had to be either thirty years old, or married before she received her inheritance.

She stepped back from the door, somehow found her way through the hotel lobby and into the ladies' room. She sank against the sink and tried to slow her breathing.

Her marriage to Jed had been arranged as part of the two companies' merger. All Jed wanted was to get control of her company shares.

Turning on the faucet, she splashed cold water on her heated face. How humiliating. Her father had actually bought a husband for her. Did he think she couldn't find a man on her own? Well, why was she surprised? J. C. Sheridan liked being in control of everything, from the boardroom to his only child's life.

Anger welled up, along with tears. He'd soon learn his reign was about to end.

Victoria Sheridan wasn't going to let her father or anyone else manipulate her, because she wasn't going to be around. She grabbed her purse and marched out of the hotel, leaving her wedding rehearsal dinner and future groom behind.

After retrieving her car from the valet, she climbed in and headed out of the parking lot. She didn't know where she was going, only that she had to get away. She would no longer do the sensible thing—the calm thing.

She had let her father convince her that marrying Jed was best for her.

But, hell, did she even love Jed? Did she even *know* him?

With only her honeymoon suitcase in the backseat, Tori stopped by the bank and withdrew the cash limit on the only credit card she had with her. The corporate credit card. When her cell phone began to ring, she turned it off and drove her car onto the freeway. North? South? Lord, she couldn't even make a decision. Finally she turned south and began driving away from San Francisco, to parts unknown…and a new life.

Chapter One

Early one spring morning, Sheriff Nate Hunter was driving on patrol, minding his own business, when he spotted her. She was a beauty. His heart skipped a beat, then set off racing. There she was in the middle of the southern Arizona desert with the sun highlighting her curves, her perfect lines. Not to mention that low-slung body and all that polished chrome.

A 1966 classic, hardtop-convertible red Corvette.

Nate slowed his breathing as well as his patrol car, made a quick U-turn, and pulled up behind the Vette. He climbed out and walked along the desert highway toward the vehicle. Outside of being dusty, she looked in mint condition. Who would leave a car like this in the middle of nowhere? California plates. He copied down the numbers and soon discovered the problem. A trail of oily substance dotted along the shoulder of the road and ended under the back of the car. He groaned as he thought about the expensive repair bill.

Nate approached the passenger side, crouched down and looked in. In the driver's seat he found a woman. Her head was tilted back, her eyes were closed and her long wheat-colored hair was draped against the white leather bucket seat.

Her slender body barely took up any room at all. His attention moved to her chest. The pink knit T-shirt fit snugly over her breasts, moving up and down with her relaxed breathing. She was asleep.

Nate rapped his knuckles against the window, but she didn't stir. He leaned closer. She was young, maybe in her midtwenties, and attractive, with a pert nose and flawless skin. His body began to react like the hot desert heat and he glanced away to compose himself.

He tapped on the window again and this time, she awoke with a start. When she opened those big, golden brown, more-striking-than-any-he'd-ever-seen eyes, Nate felt as if he'd been gut-punched.

Tori Sheridan jumped and her eyes widened at the sight of the large figure standing outside her car. Panic surged through her. "Go away," she cried, looking away from the broad-shouldered silhouette outlined by the sun.

"Ma'am, you can't park here," he called out. "It's dangerous. Do you need help?"

Tori had been on the road for three days and in that

time she'd had plenty of men who were more than willing to help her. If she'd been smart, she would have sold her Corvette and bought a sensible sedan. But she loved her car.

"If you don't leave me alone, I'm calling the police."

"Then you'll get me," he said. "I'm Sheriff Nathan Hunter."

Tori looked again and recognized the tan-colored uniform; then the badge caught the sunlight. She reached over to roll down the window. "Oh, Sheriff, I'm sorry. A woman can't be too careful."

"Well, sleeping along the side of the highway isn't exactly safe, not to mention being against the law. Would you please step out of the car, ma'am? And bring your license, registration and proof of insurance."

Tori's nervousness didn't diminish with the officer's attitude. Surely her father hadn't alerted the authorities. No, J.C. couldn't have known where she'd gone. Besides, she hadn't done anything wrong. Deciding not to irritate the sheriff any more, Tori quickly opened the glove compartment and took out the required papers. She grabbed her purse, opened the door and climbed out just as a car sped by. The blaring sound of the horn pierced the silence, and Tori felt the officer's strong grip as he jerked her away from the asphalt.

"You okay?" he asked her as he helped her to the other side of the car.

She nodded, and glanced up the road. "Shouldn't you go after that car?"

"Why? He wasn't speeding. You're the one parked on the side of the highway."

The desert sun beat down on her. It was going to be another scorcher. "Are you going to give me a ticket?"

He glared at her. "Do you deserve one?"

"No. I hadn't planned to spend the night here, Sheriff." She handed him the papers, then dug through her purse, found her wallet and tried to hand it to him.

"Take your license out, please," he asked. Never taking off his sunglasses, he examined her insurance card and registration, then did the same with her license. "You're a long way from home, Miss Sheridan."

"I guess I am." Why did she feel she'd done something wrong?

"What brings you to Arizona? Vacation or business?"

How about running away from home? "Would you believe I just got in my car and started driving?"

The sheriff glanced at her Corvette, then turned back to her. His mouth twitched as if fighting a grin. "Oh, I believe it. If I had a car like this…" He paused, then sobered. "You'll need a tow truck."

"I figured that." She sighed. "I thought it was overheating, but the car suddenly had no power when I stepped on the gas. I had to pull off the road. I was hoping that once it cooled down I could drive it again."

"I think it's more than just an overheated engine," he said and motioned for her to follow him to the back of the car.

Tori watched the well-built sheriff remove his sunglasses and she finally got a good look at his face. He wasn't classically handsome, but he had rugged good looks and piercing, silver-gray eyes. His dark hair was cut short under his wide-brimmed hat. When he looked at her, that intense gaze locked with hers, mesmerizing her.

Finally, he was the one who turned away. "This seems to be your problem." He pointed to the ground behind the car. "See the trail of oil?"

"Please don't tell me it's the transmission." She didn't have much money left.

"I'm not a mechanic, but I know a few things about cars." He paused. "It looks like your rear end."

She didn't want to sound ignorant, but she was when it came to cars. Her father's mechanic had always handled the maintenance. But now Tori's money situation gave her no choice but to ask, "Is that bad?"

"It can be complicated," the sheriff volunteered. "You need to have a mechanic look at it. This car is too special to take any chances with. You're a long way from home. Is there anyone you want me to call?"

"No!" The last thing she wanted was to go crawling back to her father. She was twenty-nine and it was time to handle things on her own. "There isn't anyone."

"How about we have your car towed into town then?"

It appeared that Tori didn't have any other options. She didn't have the money for car repairs, or much of anything else. There was less than a hundred dollars in her purse. And if she didn't want J.C. to know where she'd gone, that was all there was going to be for a while.

He was looking for her, she had no doubt. No one ran out on J. C. Sheridan without paying the consequences.

There had been dozens of cell phone messages from her father since that night she'd left town. He'd called so often she'd finally tossed her phone out the window after crossing the Arizona state line. Now, she was finally on her own.

Tori looked up at the sheriff. "I have AAA, but I could use some advice on where to take my car." She would have to use the corporate credit card for the repairs. Something she'd managed to avoid since leaving San Francisco.

"Ernie's Auto Repairs is good and he's reasonable."

"Where is Ernie located?"

"Haven," he told her. "It's a small town just about ten miles off this highway." Then he smiled, showing off straight white teeth. Something stirred in Tori's stomach.

"Don't worry, the people there are honest. Of course, you will draw some attention." The playful glint in the sheriff's silver eyes made her feel as if he were talking about her. "You have what every red-blooded man wants. A classic '66 Corvette."

"Hey, Sam, how about a couple of iced teas?" Nate called as he walked Tori Sheridan through the doors of the Good Time Café. He escorted her to the counter because that's where he usually sat most mornings for breakfast. She eased down onto a stool and he slipped onto the one next to her, unable to ignore her soft floral scent.

It was between the breakfast and lunch crowds, and the place was deserted. But his friend, Sam Price, looked a little frazzled as he hustled out of the kitchen.

"I'll be there in a second."

A stocky man, dressed in a uniform of white pants and a T-shirt with an apron tied low around his waist came into view. He set two glasses of tea in front of his only customers. "Oh, man, what a morning."

"I take it you haven't found a waitress," Nate said, knowing Sam had been handling all the customers since Nancy Turner had left town to move in with her sister.

Sam shook his head, then turned to Tori and smiled. "Good morning, ma'am."

"Sam, this is Victoria Sheridan. She had car trouble on the highway. Ernie's having a look."

"Well, it's a pleasure to meet you, Miss Sheridan." He held out his hand.

She shook it. "Please, call me Tori."

Sam's smile widened. "Well, if you aren't a breath of fresh air on this hot day."

Tori blushed and took a quick sip. "I don't know about that, but this iced tea sure is doing a nice job of cooling me off."

Nate wished he could say the same thing, but in more ways than one Tori Sheridan had been stirring up the heat since he'd stopped beside her car.

Three hours had passed since Ernie had arrived to tow her sports car. Nate had sent the pretty blonde off with the mechanic and gone back on patrol. Somehow a couple of hours later, Nate found himself stopping by the garage to check on her. When he found her sitting in the filthy repair office going through an old *Sports Illustrated* magazine, he just couldn't leave her there. He suggested they go for a cool drink.

"I thought Tori would be more comfortable here," he told Sam.

Tori had been surprised when the sheriff had showed up at the repair shop, even more so when he'd suggested a cool drink. She'd started to protest, but he'd easily convinced her they were only going a few blocks to the Good Time Café.

Tori glanced around the diner-style restaurant. It was all fifties decor, done in red and white, complete with booths and a long Formica-and-chrome counter with stools. Off in the corner was a jukebox and a small dance area. One of the first things Tori had noticed coming into the small town earlier was there wasn't a single fast-food outlet in Haven. She liked that.

"You have a nice place here, Sam."

"Thank you." He cocked an eyebrow. "You wouldn't want a job as a waitress, would you?"

Tori laughed. "Thanks for the offer, but I'm just passing through town."

"Where you headed?"

She didn't know. "Nowhere in particular. I'm just driving."

"She's got some nice wheels, too," Nate said. "A '66 Corvette. Red."

"No way." Sam laughed. "I had a Vette years ago, but mine was a black Stingray."

"And you let it go?" Nate asked, amazed.

"Let's just say it's one of the things my ex-wife decided she couldn't live without." Sam shook his head. "A woman has no business coming between a man and his car. Stay single, son, and you don't have to worry about those kinds of problems."

Tori absently rubbed her ring finger, now minus the large diamond Jed had given her. She didn't want to be accused of theft, so she'd taken the time to overnight the engagement ring back to him, along with a short note telling Jed to go to hell. She wanted nothing from either man, Jed or J.C.

Just then the door to the café opened and Ernie came in, dressed in his grease-stained overalls. "Ms. Sheridan," he called.

Tori got up and met the thirtysomething mechanic halfway across the café, holding her breath, hoping that whatever was wrong with her car, it could be fixed cheaply.

"My suspicions were right," he began. "It's the rear end."

Ernie had warned her earlier if that was the problem it wouldn't be easily solved or inexpensive. "It's going to be expensive," she sighed.

He nodded. "That and it's hard to find parts. Plus, it takes a lot of hours to put it back together."

Great. What did she do now? Go crawling back to J. C. Sheridan? No way, even if she had to sell the car.

"Can you quote me a price?" she asked.

Ernie pulled a piece of paper out of his pocket with the estimate and handed it to her. A week ago, she wouldn't have thought twice about the staggering amount, but now… And she already owed Ernie for the time it had taken him to tear apart her car.

"Thank you, Ernie. I'll come back with you now and pay you for your time." She went to the counter and took money out of her purse for her tea. Nate stopped her.

"It's on me," he said. "Let me know if I can do anything."

Can you come up with a miracle? she asked silently, and smiled. "Thank you, Sheriff, you've done a lot already." She raised her chin and followed Ernie out the door, wondering what she could get for a broken-down Corvette.

Nate wasn't sure if he'd ever see Tori Sheridan again, but found he was glad when he got a call from Ernie asking him to stop by.

When Nate got out of the patrol car the mechanic met him in front of the garage. "What's the problem?" he asked.

"Problem is right," Ernie said. "Her credit card was declined, but they also asked that it be confiscated. What do I do?"

So, Tori Sheridan might look like money, but according to her credit rating, she didn't have any. "Did you call the credit card company?"

"Yeah, first thing."

Nate hated to ask the next question. "Are there criminal charges against her?"

"No. They just said that Victoria Sheridan isn't authorized to charge on the account any longer."

Nate couldn't help but wonder who Tori had ticked off, her husband, her boyfriend, her boss? "Then, do what you're told. Take the card."

Ernie looked pained at the suggestion. "But what about the car that I took apart? And what if Tori is stranded? Man, she's such a nice lady."

As hard as he tried, Nate hadn't been able to stop thinking about Tori Sheridan. But he didn't need any more on his plate right now. He had to stay focused on his job, not on the pretty stranger who'd come to town needing help. He didn't listen to his own common sense; instead he walked into Ernie's office to talk with Tori.

"I've got bad news," Nate began. "Your credit card was declined."

Her honey-brown eyes widened as she jumped up from the chair. "That can't be. There's a twenty-five-thousand-dollar credit line on that card."

Nate couldn't comprehend having that kind of money at hand. "Maybe I should rephrase that and say that you just aren't authorized to use the card any longer."

"What?" Her voice was hoarse. "No, he wouldn't do that to me."

His protective instincts kicked in. "You sure there isn't anyone you can contact? Could be a phone call would straighten this out." What man in his right mind could strand this woman without any money?

"I wouldn't give him the satisfaction," she said angrily, then looked at Nate. "Oh, no! I don't have any money. Not even enough to pay Ernie."

"Then Ernie will have to hold on to your car until you can come up with the payment."

Tori looked embarrassed. "That's going to take a while, but I promise I'll get him the money."

"I believe you. Besides, that car of yours is worth a lot more than the price of the repairs. I'm sure Ernie wouldn't mind holding it in the shop for a week or so. Would you, Ernie?"

"Oh, no, Tori," the mechanic said. "It's a beautiful car. I just hope I get the chance to fix it."

Tori nodded. "I'll have to let you know on that."

This was where Nate usually got himself into trouble. He'd done his duty as sheriff and helped her off the highway. He didn't owe Victoria Sheridan any more than that.

"Do you have any idea what you're going to do?"

"Not a clue," she answered dejectedly. "You wouldn't have an empty jail cell?"

"Do you have enough for bus fare home?"

Tori's pretty eyes suddenly lost their sparkle. "That's the last place I want to go."

That was when an idea came to him. He excused himself and headed down the street, back to the café to have a talk with Sam.

He walked into the empty restaurant and found his friend clearing a table. "Hey, Sam, you still need a waitress?"

"You know I do," the older man said and carried a stack of dirty plates into the kitchen. When he returned he poured two glasses of iced tea and handed one to Nate. "Why? You need to moonlight to save up more money to buy the ranch?"

Nate didn't need to be reminded of how he'd been scraping together every dime he had to be able to bid on his old homestead.

"I don't think I'd do well on tips," he joked. "I've given too many people around here tickets. No, I have someone else in mind. What do you think about hiring Tori?"

Sam cocked an eyebrow.

"It seems her credit card got declined. She's stranded here."

Sam shook his head. "They see you coming, don't they? The soft touch."

So he'd helped a few people and gotten a reputation. "Hey, I just figured since you needed a waitress and Tori needs a job, that it would be good for the both of you. But if you're not interested…"

"I didn't say I wasn't interested. How do I know she's reliable?"

"You don't," Nate answered. "You'll have to take a chance. But what other choice do you have? There hasn't been anyone else willing to work here." Nate wasn't sure that Tori wanted the job, either. "So, how 'bout it?"

Before Sam could answer, the woman in question walked through the door. She saw them at the counter and with her shoulders squared, she came toward them. "Sam, do you have a pay phone I can use?"

"In back, next to the rest rooms."

Nate waited until she walked off. "Well, do you want a waitress or not?"

Sam breathed a long sigh. "I guess I could give her a try."

Nate wasn't finished, and he wondered if his next favor would push their friendship too far. "What do you say about letting Tori stay in the room upstairs?"

Sam didn't say a word for a long time, then grinned. "Man, she's really gotten to you. Sure, why not? If anything, I'd like to have her hang around just to see what develops between the two of you."

Nate got up. "Nothing. I'd do the same for anyone."

"I know. That's your problem, Nate. You give to everyone. When are you going to learn to take?"

Nate froze. He'd learned all right. And he'd been paying for his selfishness ever since. "I will when I get the ranch back."

Tori stood in front of the black pay phone for a long time. She didn't want to call her father, but what choice did she have now? If she had thought this through before leaving town she wouldn't be in this mess. She didn't have her ATM card with her, and besides she was already sharing a joint account with Jed. The one credit card that had been in her small evening bag was the corporate one. Her other bank cards were at home and there was no way to get to them. And if she called the credit card company it would take too long to issue her a new one. So she had no choice but to call J.C. She had picked up the phone and begun to dial when she heard her name called out.

She turned to see Nate Hunter walking toward her. His large frame easily filled the narrow hallway. He looked intimidating in his khaki sheriff's uniform, but his authoritative demeanor actually made her feel safe.

"I think I may have a solution to your problem," he said.

It would take a lot to solve her problems, but she hung up the phone. "Did you find a bag of money in my car?"

He smiled and tiny lines crinkled around his silver eyes. Her stomach suddenly did a somersault. She doubted it had anything to do with being hungry.

"I wish. As he mentioned before, Sam needs a waitress for the morning shift."

Tori blinked. A waitress? She'd never waited tables. "I don't have any experience."

"Sam's willing to give you a try. And I hear the tips are pretty good."

Tori felt her insecurities surface but she pushed them aside. Heck, she'd never worked for anyone besides her father. Waitressing had to be easier than working for J.C. "It sounds wonderful, and thank you, Sheriff."

"Please, call me Nate."

"Thank you, Nate, but I don't have a place to stay and no money…"

"That's not a problem, either." His smile widened into a grin and she could barely manage her next breath. What was wrong with her? Just days ago she had planned to marry Jed.

"If you're not too particular about the decor," he began, "Sam says you can stay in the room upstairs. Then you can work and save up enough money to pay Ernie for your car and parts. I'm sure he'll let you make payments."

Tori had trouble handling all this kindness, these people who would accept a stranger into their town, into their homes. She blinked back tears of emotion. "I don't know what to say."

"I think yes is a good start."

"Yes, I'll do it. I don't know how I'll repay you."

The sheriff stepped closer. "I can think of one way."

She managed to swallow the dryness in her throat, almost afraid to ask. "What is that?"

"Let me drive your car once it's fixed."

She found herself laughing for the first time in days. "You got yourself a deal. And Sam's got himself a waitress."

Chapter Two

Fighting back a gasp, Tori glanced around her temporary home. The sheriff hadn't lied when he'd said the room wasn't much to look at. The walls were dingy beige and the floor was a worn vinyl covered partly by a mud-brown throw rug. At least there was a bed, or more accurately a frame and mattress.

Next to the only window sat a scarred dresser layered with several coats of paint, the last a pea-green. Along the far wall were several boxes labeled as restaurant supplies.

"What have I gotten myself into?" she breathed as she eyed the mass of cobwebs along the ceiling. Just then her appraisal was interrupted by the sound of footsteps on the stairs.

With a loud knock, Nate Hunter walked through the door. He nodded in greeting and held up her small suitcase. "I thought you might need this."

Tori doubted her honeymoon trousseau would be practical for her stay in Haven. She blushed, recalling the skimpy silk-and-satin unmentionables that filled the bag, guaranteed to lure any man into her bed. Just days ago, Tori had had plans to seduce her new husband in the tropical island of Kauai, Hawaii.

Now, the only ideas she had for her ex-fiancé could get her arrested. And Jed wasn't worth it. Tori bit back her anger and smiled at the sheriff. "Thank you. It's not much, but it's all I have." With her quick departure and limited funds, she'd only managed a little clothes shopping at the discount stores.

"You're welcome." He glanced around the room. "Oh, boy, it's worse than I remembered."

Tori wanted to agree, but she was too grateful to have a place to stay.

"It's fine," she said. "Really, this is all I need. Besides, Sam has been nice enough to let me stay here. With a little cleaning…"

"It will still look bad," Nate said ruefully.

Tori remained silent as she glanced inside the tiny bathroom that contained a stall shower, sink and toilet. She grimaced at the thought of the last time it had been cleaned.

Get a grip, girl. Tori looked back at the sheriff. "Like I said, a good cleaning and this will do just fine."

Her only other alternative was to call her father. If she did, she'd be sleeping in a five-star hotel tonight. But she'd have to pay a price. No. She wasn't going to give the man any more control over her. It was past time she handled her own life. Starting now.

"Do you think Sam could spare some cleaning supplies?" she asked.

"Sure." Nate began to roll up his uniform sleeves. "Don't touch a thing until I get back with some strong disinfectant and we'll make this place livable."

"Sheriff, no. There's no need for you to help me. I'm sure you have more important things to do."

"I know I don't have to." His piercing eyes bored into hers and her throat suddenly went dry. "As for more important things to do…" He checked his watch. "I got off duty twenty minutes ago. And I have capable deputies who'll call me if they can't handle things. Now, I'm going to get those cleaning supplies from Sam and help you. Is that all right with you?"

Tori swallowed hard, never so aware of the close quarters—or so aware that Sheriff Nate Hunter was a good-looking man with a killer dimple in his chin. It would be too easy to lean on him, and the last thing she wanted or needed was Prince Charming. No more fairy tales. If anyone was going to rescue her, she would do it herself—but maybe a little help with the cleaning wouldn't hurt.

She finally nodded. "Just so you know, I'm adding more time to when you drive my car."

A slow sexy grin appeared and her breathing stopped. "I'm easy," he said. "I'll work for Vette time."

She doubted anything about this man was easy. "Don't get too excited. First, I have to pay for the repairs. So you better hope I make some tips."

The sheriff's intent gaze moved over her and suddenly her cotton shirt and white capris felt as if they'd disappeared. "Oh, I have no doubt you'll do very well," he said, then turned and walked out the door.

Tori sank onto the stool and let out a long breath. Waitress. Tips. Car repairs. How fast her life had changed. A sudden sadness washed over her as she recalled that just days ago she was to have been married. Now she was flirting with another man.

The Sheridan-Foster wedding was supposed to be San Francisco's society event of the year. Deep inside, Tori had never felt right about the marriage. She realized now that she'd never loved Jed, at least not the way a woman should love the man she planned to spend the rest of her life with.

It dawned on her that she'd let her father brainwash her into thinking she and Jed were perfect for each other. J.C. had said they had so much in common and Jed had been just as convincing. In truth, the marriage would have been advantageous for J. C. Sheridan and his business dealings. As usual, his daughter's feelings were his last concern. Had her father ever loved her, or was her only value her stock shares? That hurt worst of all. Suddenly, tears filled her eyes and she couldn't seem to stop the sobs that shook her body.

Nate heard Tori's soft sobbing even before he found his way up the stairs with the bucket and mop. He wasn't quite sure what he should do. He knew from experience with his sister that Tori probably wouldn't want anyone to see her cry. But Tori was all alone. Would she go back to the man who had caused the sadness in her big brown eyes? Those sparkling golden-hued eyes had been Nate's undoing, not to mention her pouty, kissable lips and thick, wheat-colored hair.

Nate quickly shook away the direction of his thoughts. He was the sheriff and should be checking for outstanding warrants, or if she was on a missing persons list rather than fantasizing about her.

It had turned out she had a spotless record; she'd never even had a traffic ticket. She lived in an exclusive area of San Francisco and drove an expensive car. Victoria Sheridan had high society written all over her. So why didn't she have any money on her? Or anyone to call for help? Another snuffle came from the other side of the door and Nate's chest tightened. He wasn't an expert but he'd bet someone had broken her heart. A warning signal went up in his brain.

Stay away from her. You can't take on another problem, especially not a female with problems!

Nate had given his heart once and it had been shattered. Allison Denton, the girl he'd loved all through college, had walked out on him when he'd needed her the most. She'd suddenly lost interest in him when he was no longer headed toward a pro-football career.

Since then Nate had guarded his heart but good. Yet he knew he couldn't turn away from someone who needed his help. He made a stomping sound on the porch before he opened the door and walked inside. "Looks like we're all set."

Tori had managed to brush away the tears, though her red eyes were proof of her misery. But nothing took away from her beauty.

"Look, Sheriff, you've helped me so much already, I can't expect…"

"As I mentioned before, it's Nate," he reminded her as he set down the bucket and went to her. "Tori, I know this place isn't a perfect solution—"

"No, it isn't that," she interrupted. "It's just there are things that… I can't talk about…"

He arched an eyebrow and jammed his hands into his pockets, fighting to keep from reaching for her. "And that's your business. I just figure there's a guy involved. And if you had a fight, shouldn't you try and talk to him?"

She stiffened. "Whatever relationship I had in the past is over," Tori said sternly. "And talking about it isn't going to change anything." She stepped back from him. "So thanks for the cleaning supplies. I can handle things now."

Nate decided not to push it any further. He made his way to the sink to fill the bucket.

She came after him. "What are you doing?"

The hell if he knew. "Around here it's called being neighborly. Let it go at that."

Tori looked at him with those huge eyes and he had trouble keeping his mind on what he was doing.

"Do you always get your way?" she asked.

That was a loaded question since he wanted to get his way with her. "One can always hope."

It seemed impossible, but in less than a few hours they'd made the place livable. The walls still needed paint, but at least the rooms were clean. With the fresh linen Sam had brought up, Tori had made the bed so she had a place to sleep that night.

Nate stood back and surveyed his work. "It's still not the Ritz, but I think you'll be comfortable here."

Proudly, Tori glanced around the clean, orderly room. The bed was neat and tidy and her clothes were arranged in the dresser drawers. The window was covered with a mini-slat blind, now missing the layer of dirt. The kitchen area had a chipped counter with two stools, a cabinet with mismatched dishes and a drawer of assorted flatware.

"This seems like paradise to me. Remember, I slept in my car last night."

"Which I'm going to advise you not to do again," Nate warned her. "You were lucky."

"I'm lucky in a lot of ways. I have a place to live and a job." She frowned. "But, Nate, I've never been a waitress before."

He shrugged. "Sam's pretty easygoing. He's not going to yell at you if that's what you think. Besides, I have a feeling you'll catch on fast." His gaze met hers. "What did you do in San Francisco?"

Tori didn't want to say too much about her past life. It was nice that no one here knew her father. "I was an executive assistant for a software company."

He cocked an eyebrow. "Well, there aren't any software companies around here. The closest would be in Tucson."

"Believe me, I'm happy to have this job. I'm just nervous because…" She had never worked for anyone but her father, she thought. Lord, she'd led a sheltered life. "I'm new in town."

"Well, I grew up here and everyone is pretty friendly."

Including the town's handsome sheriff, Tori thought. "We'll see tomorrow morning when I mess up the food orders."

His gaze grew softer. "Believe me, once you smile no one's going to care what you put in front of them."

At five forty-five the next morning, Tori checked her red-trimmed white uniform in the mirror. The fifties-style outfit had a fitted bodice and an A-line skirt that hit her just about at her knees. She pulled her hair into a ponytail and brushed her bangs across her forehead. On her feet, she wore the pair of new white tennis shoes she had purchased the day before.

If her father could see her now. No doubt he would feel this job was beneath a Sheridan. She might have thought the same thing a few weeks ago, but now she needed to survive in the real world.

Tori released a long breath to relax, but it didn't calm her. She left the rest room and went to the counter where Sam, dressed in white uniform pants and T-shirt, was checking the coffee.

"You ready to start?"

"No!" she said. "I can't remember everything you showed me."

"I don't expect you to," he said. "There's a lot to know." He frowned at her. "Just remember to call out each order to me, except for the drinks. You get those. When the customers come in, just keep the coffee flowing. You'll do fine."

Tori nodded as Sam walked over and unlocked the café door. Within seconds several men came in and called out in greeting to Sam. She put on a smile to hide her terror. The men removed their cowboy hats and found seats at the counter.

"Hey, everyone, this is Tori. And don't give her a bad time. I'd like her to stay around awhile."

"Good morning, gentlemen," she piped in as her face flamed. "How about some coffee?" She grabbed the glass pot and brought it to the patrons, filling the mugs that already lined the counter, and then took out her pen and notepad. "What would you like for breakfast?"

The orders came fast. Just as Sam had taught her, she

called each order back to the kitchen. More customers arrived and squeezed into the booths. That was when Tori realized that she was out of shape. The two days a week she'd spent in the gym hadn't readied her for this workout. She covered what seemed like miles between taking orders, refilling coffee cups and clearing tables. There were a few mishaps—broken dishes, mixed-up orders—but everyone was patient and friendly. Finally, around nine-thirty, the crowd thinned and Sam told her to take a break.

"But the tables need to be cleared," she told him.

He waved her off. "They'll wait."

He filled two mugs and pointed to the stool at the counter. She sat, took a long sip of the warm liquid and sighed.

"Well, you ready to quit?"

"No. Why? Are you ready to fire me?"

"Not hardly. You did great. You're bringing in business."

His praise was a stimulant to her ego. "You mean this morning's crowd wasn't the usual?"

He shrugged. "Some were, but more came in to see the pretty new lady in town." He took a sip of coffee. "Don't get me wrong, I have a good weekday breakfast crowd, but Saturday isn't usually this busy."

Before Tori could comment, the door opened and Nate Hunter walked in. He looked big and sexy dressed in faded jeans and a light blue Western-cut shirt and boots, even more handsome than in his uniform, if that were possible. And it was.

He smiled and she realized she'd missed him since he'd left the apartment yesterday. "Good morning," she said, starting to stand, until his warm hand touched her on the shoulder.

"No, don't get up. I'll get my own coffee." He smiled at Tori. "Looks like you survived your first morning."

"Yes, I did," she said proudly. "Everyone was so nice and patient with me."

His grin broadened as he leaned against the counter. "I bet that was a real hardship for them."

Sam chuckled. "Duke Hastings nearly tripped over his tongue when Tori smiled at him."

"Which one was Duke?" she asked.

"He sat at the end of the counter," Sam offered. "The skinny guy in the red shirt with the stutter. I should have charged him rent. He hung around for nearly an hour."

"He was nice," she said, remembering how shy he'd been. "And I spilled coffee on his eggs."

Both men laughed. "I bet that made his day."

"Well, he made mine." Tori pulled the folded bills from her pocket, drawing Sam's and Nate's attention. "He tips very well."

The following evening Nate sat on his mother's porch enjoying the cool breeze. It was too hot to stay inside his apartment above the garage. Besides, he liked the view along peaceful Grove Street. He tipped his chair on its back legs, placed his boots on the white-spindled railing, and ran a razor-sharp knife over the small block of wood he held in his hands. His long-practiced strokes peeled away the unwanted layers, just as his grandfather had taught him years ago, making a figure take shape.

He thought back to the first time his grandpa had told him he was old enough to handle a knife, that had been the same summer he'd gotten to ride in the Double H Ranch's roundup.

Over four generations of Hunters had lived and died on that land until the bank took the last of the Hunter's Haven homestead away two months after his father, Edward Hunter, died. That tragedy hadn't mattered to the bank officer. He'd foreclosed and sold the land out from under the family.

Luckily, his father had had life insurance so Betty Hunter and her family had been able to buy a modest home in town. It wasn't the same. Nate didn't like thinking about that time in his life and all the mistakes he'd made. And the last angry words he'd spoken to his dad before he'd walked out. Even ten years later, the guilt still haunted him. And next month, he hoped, he was going to get back some of what the Hunter family had lost.

Nate heard his name called and looked up to see old Otis Carl wave as he walked down the street. He called out in greeting, hoping the eighty-year-old didn't want to stop and talk. Not that he didn't like to visit with neighbors, but tonight he needed some alone time. He'd been on edge for the last few days. He blamed it on the heat, or maybe it was Haven's pretty new resident and thoughts of what she was doing tonight. Damn. He pushed aside the intruding image of Tori.

It was the upcoming land auction that he needed to focus on. The Double H was being sold next month and he couldn't stop worrying about scraping enough money together to make a competitive bid on part of the old homestead. The Double H rightfully belonged to the Hunters, and he planned to make it theirs once again.

He'd sure feel more secure if he had extra cash. If only his brother could pay him back the money Nate had loaned him to start up his construction business. Immediately, Nate felt guilty. He'd given that money to Shane three years ago with no strings attached. Besides, his younger brother didn't have it to give to him. Everything he had was tied up in the Haven's Paradise development. Shane probably wouldn't show a profit until the first phase of homes were about to break ground. If there were no delays that still would be a few months off.

Nate knew his brother would help him if he could, he'd already offered to help remodel the ranch house. With luck that would happen next month, after the auction. Then, finally, Nate would be able to think about his life and his future. His mother was settled now, his sister would graduate from college next spring and Shane's business was off the ground.

It was his time. It was time for him to start living his dreams. And Nate only wanted ten sections of land from the original homestead, Hunter's Haven, the Double H Ranch. He smiled, remembering the story: his great-great-grandmother, Rebecca, had named the valley as soon as she'd arrived, as Jacob Hunter's new bride, in this land surrounded by majestic mountains. Now Nate had a chance to regain some part of his heritage. He'd begin with a small herd of cattle, and maybe he'd train some saddle horses. It wouldn't be an easy life. The ranch was fifteen miles out of town, but not completely isolated. He didn't want to be alone, but it would take a special woman to want to live on a ranch. Again he thought about Tori.

Just then a patrol car came down the street, stopped in front of the house and Ryan Clark climbed out. Ryan was one of the newest deputies, not a year out of the sheriff's academy.

"Well, there goes my night off," Nate murmured. "Hey, Ryan. Is there a problem?"

"I stopped Kurt Easton about an hour ago."

Great. "Just tell me you had good cause."

Ryan nodded. "He was doing eighty on the old county road."

Nate knew Easton wouldn't be happy. He'd had run-ins with the lawyer and city councilman before. There was a time when Kurt Easton was a frequent patron of the local bars. A few years back Nate had caught the councilor staggering in the parking lot of just such an establishment toward his car. The councilman had intended to drive home. With his wife safely behind the wheel, Nate had let the man off with a warning and the belligerent Easton's agreement to get himself some help. Nate hoped he had taken the advice.

"Was he under the influence?"

The deputy shook his head. "At first I thought so. He seemed a little lethargic, but passed the field sobriety test. He wasn't happy and proceeded to read me the riot act about how he knew his rights." Ryan straightened. "I followed procedure by the book. I took a step back and I informed the councilman to get in his car, or I'd take him into custody."

Nate continued to work his knife. "Did you take him into custody?"

"No, he climbed in his car, but before he drove off, he told me to tell you that he'd be in your office the first thing in the morning to file a complaint."

"Okay. I'll handle it, Ryan."

The deputy stepped up onto the porch. "Sheriff, I swear I went by the book."

Nate had had several run-ins with Easton. His family had been in the valley nearly as long as the Hunters and about half that time they'd been feuding. At every opportunity Kurt Easton reminded Nate that his family had lost everything.

"I know you did, Ryan. I'll take care of it in the morning when my shift starts."

The deputy looked relieved. He was happy the sheriff would have the responsibility of dealing with one of the most prominent men in town. "Thanks, Nate."

Nate kept slicing at the block of wood. "Just because he's a councilman doesn't give him any special privileges. He broke the law. Now, get back on patrol. You can start by driving by the construction site just to make sure things are quiet. You were off last week when someone threw a party down there. It was probably kids, but I'd like you to keep a close watch."

Ryan nodded. "Sure. 'Night, Sheriff," he called as he headed back to the patrol car.

Nate watched him go, knowing what he had in store in the morning. There was no doubt that the fifty-something lawyer would be waiting for him, hoping he could stir up some trouble for a Hunter.

"Was that Ryan Clark?" His mother's voice broke the silence of the quiet night.

Nate glanced up as the tall slender woman came out the screen door. Betty Hunter had turned fifty-five this year, and although she had a few gray hairs mixed in with her light brown, she looked years younger. She'd taken up running ten years ago after her husband had died suddenly of a heart attack. Along with a healthy diet and teaching at the elementary school, that had helped to keep her youthful figure.

"Yeah, he had a question," Nate said, running his knife over the wood in the dimming light.

"It's finally starting to cool off." She took the chair next to his. "What are you starting on now?"

"I'm not sure," he said, though already a design was forming in his head.

"Whatever you carve, it will be beautiful." She smiled. "I've told you a hundred times, you should sell those figures."

"Then I wouldn't enjoy it as much. How could I relax if I had a production line going?"

"I'm not talking about a production line. But you could make extra money, maybe it could help you with your goal." They both knew she was talking about the ranch.

He stopped his knife. "I'm sheriff, Mom. I don't have the time."

"Nathan..." she began, then paused. "I know you have a lot on your plate right now, probably too much. And maybe that's my fault. I've relied on you too much since your father's death."

"Mom, I only did what Dad would have wanted. You needed me. Shane and Emily were still kids."

"But you gave up so much. And you've helped Shane start his business and Emily..." Her voice grew hoarse with emotion. "I never could have afforded college for her without your help."

"I wanted Em to have the same chance to go to school that I did, even if she plans to go work in Hollywood."

"There's still time to change her mind, but God knows she's stubborn," his mother said, turning her attention back to him. "I only wish I could help you have your dream."

He didn't like it when his mother got sentimental. He stood. "I'm happy, Mom. I've got a good job and family."

At one time he'd had a lot of dreams. Nate thought

back to college, when he was a wide receiver trying to make it to the pros. He nearly did, too, until he'd gotten hurt, then suddenly he wasn't in demand any longer.

So the injured hometown boy returned home, but only for as long as it took his leg to heal. Even when his father had asked him to stay and help out with the ranch, Nate wanted out of Haven, and he took off to the sheriff's academy. No sooner had he graduated and was about to take a job in the Phoenix area, than his father died of a heart attack. Nate rushed home to help his mother and younger brother and sister. But he couldn't keep the bank from taking the Double H. They all moved into town and he took the deputy's job. Four years ago he'd run for sheriff. Maybe if the townspeople had known he'd been a selfish bastard, he wouldn't have won so easily.

Over the last few years, he'd realized that he wouldn't want to live anywhere else. His family's roots were deep in this valley and he wanted the ranch back. He owed that much to his father, especially since he was the reason Ed Hunter had mortgaged the property in the first place—to help pay for his son's college education.

His mother's voice interrupted his reverie. "What about the Double H?"

Yes, that was his one remaining dream. In its rundown condition, the old place wasn't worth much to anyone but him. Nate hoped to be the only bidder at the auction, praying he could get the ranch pretty cheap. Funny, for years all he'd wanted was to travel the world. Now he couldn't think about living anywhere else.

His thoughts returned to Tori. Her sudden arrival had brightened his mundane life. But that was about as far as he was going to take it. She'd probably hang around a few days, then call a friend and be gone. It was a good thing. A woman like Tori wouldn't be happy in a small town like Haven. He'd bet his next paycheck that she was San Francisco society. Just look at the car she drove. Still, he was impressed by how hard she'd worked to clean up Sam's apartment, and how she hadn't once complained after her first grueling day waiting tables at the café. And he hadn't missed how good she looked in her uniform, nor had any of the other male patrons.

"I hear there's a visitor in town," his mother said.

Nate shrugged, not wanting to show too much interest. "Tori Sheridan. She's staying until her car is repaired."

"Is that why she's working for Sam?"

Nate frowned. "You seem to have a lot of questions about someone who's just passing through."

"Mary Orwell told me about the new waitress." She shrugged. "It isn't often we get new people in town."

"Mom, she's won't be around long. Tori has a life back in San Francisco." And probably a man who cared about her, he thought.

"Maybe she'll stay for a while if she meets someone special."

"I know what you're thinking, Mom. And I'm going to put an end to your hopes. I'm not interested in getting involved with anyone. I helped Tori when she was stranded on the highway and helped her get a job with

Sam. That's all. Even if I were interested, I have nothing to offer a woman right now."

"Son, you have a lot to offer," his mother insisted.

"Oh, yeah. An apartment over my mother's garage, and soon all my money will be tied up in buying and restoring a run-down ranch. Besides, it's been so long since I've gone out on a date, I probably wouldn't remember how to carry on a decent conversation."

His mother stood and kissed him on the cheek. "Since when is conversation the main priority?" With a wink, she turned and walked back into the house.

Nate groaned in frustration as he leaned against the pillar and stared out at the quiet street. For the past two days, he'd fought to keep his mind off Tori Sheridan and had failed miserably.

For the first time in a long time, he *was* interested. But something told him that she was running from someone. His protective instincts kicked in where Tori was concerned, making him want to slug the guy who had caused her pain and made her cry. It would be wise for him just to back away and stay clear of the pretty stranger.

But this time Nate wasn't thinking about doing the wise thing. All he could think about at this moment was having breakfast at the Good Time Café tomorrow.

Chapter Three

There was standing room only in the café Monday morning. Customers were lined up at the door for a vacant seat in the packed dining room. Tori was getting faster at her job, calling out orders like a pro, able to carry several plates at one time and clear tables efficiently, but it didn't seem to help thin the crowd.

They kept coming in.

She moved through the mass quickly, carrying hot food to the patrons, wondering if it were possible to wear out a single pair of tennis shoes in three days. On one of her trips back to the kitchen she caught sight of a familiar figure. It was Nate Hunter. With coffeepot in hand, he was refilling mugs for the men seated at the counter. She hadn't seen him since her first day at work and couldn't help but watch the popular sheriff joke and trade small talk with customers. His dark hair was still damp from the shower and his jaw smooth from a recent shave. Dressed in his starched khaki uniform, he looked way too good for this early in the morning.

Tori blew out a tired breath, making her damp curls dance from her forehead, and feeling more than a little wilted in the heat. Suddenly Nate turned his silver-eyed gaze on her and her pulse picked up as a flush rushed to her cheeks. He tossed her a flirty wink, but she refused to be entirely charmed. She hurriedly began to fill water glasses, reminding herself that she'd sworn off men.

It was all about survival, both financial and emotional. She had no time to think about the sexy sheriff of Haven. She walked to a booth and set four glasses on the table. Wiping her wet hands on her apron, Tori pulled out her pad and pencil.

"What can I get for you gentlemen?" she asked. The group was all dressed in jeans and chambray shirts and thick-soled work boots. They had to be construction workers.

"How about if you let me take you away from all this?" The suggestion came from the youngest in the group, a cute blond boy who couldn't be any older than eighteen.

Tori had had several invitations to go out since she'd started working four days ago, and she'd learned to handle them. "Sorry, I'm a little busy right now." All of the men laughed, except the young guy who'd made the suggestion.

"Then I'll come back later. What time do you get off?" His expression told her he was serious.

"Thank you for the invitation, but I don't have much time for a social life. And if I don't get this order in, Sam will fire me," she fibbed. "So what will it be, boys?"

Finally they gave her their orders, and she walked away carrying the menus. "Four specials, two scrambled, two over easy and a side of flapjacks," Tori called out to Sam, and clipped the order on the rounder by the kitchen window where he stood at the grill. She picked up the order that was ready to go. With the plates in hand, Tori turned to find the kid from the booth standing in her path.

"I meant what I said about wanting to take you out," he said.

Oh, boy. He wasn't going to go away easily. "Look…"

"Matt. Matt Hillenbrand."

"Matt…I really can't talk right now." She tried to move around him, but he wouldn't let her. "And if you don't let me by to serve breakfast, several people in the room are going to be very angry."

"Then tell me when we can get together."

She sighed. "We can't."

He looked surprised and hurt. "Is it because you think I'm too young?"

Tori heard her name being called, the order bell sounded, but this boy wasn't going to let her be. "No. It's because—"

"Tori, is there a problem?"

She was glad and angry at the same time, at the sound of Nate's voice. "No." She kept her gaze on Matt. "Matt and I were just coming to an understanding." She knew that the older guys in the booth had probably dared him to come after her.

Tori glanced up at Nate. His stern-sheriff look told her he wasn't convinced. "Hey, Matt. How's the new job working out?"

"Just fine, Sheriff."

"Good," Nate said as he placed a protective arm across her back and moved in closer. Tori could feel the heat from his solid body as he pulled her against him. Suddenly, she had trouble holding on to the plates in her hands. Oh, no, he was acting as if there was something between the two of them.

"Now, why don't you let Tori do her job?" Nate asked. "As you can see she's pretty busy right now."

The young man glanced first at Nate then at Tori. "Seems she's busy all right," Matt said, under his breath. Finally, Matt moved aside so Tori could pass. Somehow she managed to walk to the waiting table and hand out the food. After taking payment from table three, she glanced over her shoulder to see that the teenager was still talking with Nate.

Tori decided to go back to the kitchen by the long way. She picked up some more orders and when she turned around, Matt had returned to the booth and Nate was gone. She found she was a little upset that he felt he had to handle the situation for her. She didn't want him to keep rescuing her. She definitely didn't want to be dependent on him. When she brought food to Matt and his friends none of the men said a word besides thanks, but they left a hearty tip.

By the time the breakfast rush ended, Tori was more than ready for a break. Never again in her life-time would she complain to a waitress about service. Not after the many times she had messed up orders and bills, not to mention spilling coffee on innocent customers.

She glanced in the mirror over the counter. Her hair was a mass of curls thanks to the humidity. Her makeup was nonexistent, her uniform looked as though she'd been in a food fight. If her father could see how unkempt she was right now, he wouldn't claim her.

She doubted J.C. would claim her anyway, since she'd gone against his wishes. Sadness washed over her. She'd spent her entire life trying to win her father's love, hoping he'd notice the lonely child he'd left with numerous nannies or sent away to boarding schools. By the time she'd reached college, she'd finally realized there was no pleasing J. C. Sheridan.

So she'd decided she would make a life for herself and do what she'd wanted to do. She'd majored in child development so she could teach young children. Then, surprisingly, after graduation, J.C. had asked her to come and work with him. Once again, the child in her wanted her father, on any terms. She'd even convinced herself she loved a man she hardly knew to please him. No more. She wasn't going to beg for her father's love anymore. In the end, she'd only end up getting hurt again.

Sam came out of the kitchen and Tori quickly masked her downbeat mood with a smile. He sat down on the stool beside her. "Busy morning," he said.

"No kidding."

"I saw you had a little trouble earlier. Has it happened before?"

She shrugged. "It wasn't bad. I think Matt was just trying to impress his friends."

"I take it Nate set him straight."

"Yeah, he did." Tori wasn't used to men coming to her rescue. A part of her was flattered he was there for her, but she didn't want to depend on him.

"Matt Hillenbrand isn't a bad kid, just a little spoiled," Sam said. "He went off to college and partied a little too hearty so his dad made him get a job to learn some responsibility. He's been working for Hunter Construction Company."

Tori frowned. "Nate owns a construction company?"

"No, his younger brother, Shane, does, but I think Nate has invested enough money into the business to be a partner. Early on the company had some rough times, but now there's a lot of new construction in the area. Hunter Construction won the bid on a new housing project at the north end of town, and Shane has had to hire a larger crew. That's why we've been getting a big crowd in the mornings. A lot of the workers are from out of town and are staying at the Lazy 8 Motel." He smiled. "It's good for business here and all over town."

Tori couldn't stop thinking about Nate's family. "So the Hunters are pretty close." She tried to keep the envy out of her voice.

Sam nodded. "Yeah, the four are, Nate, Betty, Shane and the youngest, Emily, who is away at college right now." Sam sighed. "Betty went through a lot after her husband died. The whole family did."

"How long ago did he die?"

"Oh, let's see, Ed's been gone about ten years now. It was just a year after Nate graduated from Arizona State. Back then the boy was Haven's hero. ASU football team's star wide receiver. He had speed and unbelievable hands and was headed for the NFL…then he was injured."

Sam shook his head. "After that, the pros changed their minds about Nate's abilities, so he came home to recuperate. Ed was happy to have his son back to help out with the ranch. Nate had other ideas, and decided he wanted to go to the Central Arizona Law Officers Training Academy. He graduated and took a deputy's job there just when Ed had a massive heart attack and died. That was when Nate returned home and stayed." Sam shook his head. "It was rough on the family. Not only had they lost Ed, they lost the ranch and had to move into town. Nate took a job here and a few years ago got elected sheriff. And as you can see, he's a popular guy."

"I didn't mean for him to have to fill coffee cups."

Sam chuckled. "Don't worry about it. I have several customers who help me out on occasion, Nate is just one of them. He's like that, always helping a friend or a neighbor."

Tori doubted she could find anyone in town who didn't think highly of Sheriff Nathan Hunter. She had yet to find any faults in the man. Definitely not in his dark, sexy looks. He was charming, and his body was perfect. Her stomach fluttered, but she pushed the feeling aside. She wasn't interested. She couldn't afford to be.

Tori realized that Sam had been talking to her. "Sorry, Sam. What did you say?"

He smiled. "Not used to these long hours?"

"I've worked long hours, just not standing on my feet. I admit that at my last job I spent a lot of time sitting in front of the computer."

He cocked an eyebrow. "Something tells me you're way overqualified for this job."

"I'm not when I need money," she said, realizing she had trouble getting the words out. Sam had been nicer to her than her own father, and with no questions asked.

He studied her for a long time, then placed his hand over hers. "I know I seem like a stranger, but if you ever need to talk I'm a pretty good listener."

Tori's eyes welled up. "Thank you. You've been so kind to me already."

"You may not think that after I ask a big favor. Could you put in a few extra hours in the afternoons?"

She couldn't help but smile. "Does that mean I'm not such a bad waitress?"

"You're a great waitress. I wish I had a dozen more like you. You don't know how glad I am I took Nate's suggestion and hired you. You work hard and make no complaints."

"You work hard, too, Sam."

"But I'm crazy."

They both laughed and Tori realized it had been a long time since she'd felt lighthearted.

"You have a nice laugh, Tori Sheridan."

"Thank you."

He stood. "When the high-school kids come in this afternoon, have fun, but don't let them get away with anything. Their hormones are going crazy, but they know my rules. Most of the time they're pretty good kids, and they like my music."

Tori had checked out the music in the jukebox and found the selections included only hits from the fifties and sixties. "Do they have a choice?"

"Yeah, they can go hang out at the Pizza Palace and listen to country and western or that hip-hop junk."

Later that day, Tori soon learned that Sam was a softy when it came to kids. Dozens of them came in and greeted him affectionately. Teenage girls gathered around the jukebox and dropped quarters in to hear Elvis's "Jailhouse Rock." Then surprisingly they began to swing dance. Several of the boys came up to sit at the counter and Sam introduced them to Tori.

She was surprised when the boys began shooting questions at her. One boy, Randy, asked, "How did you get a Corvette?"

"I got it as a gift when I graduated college," she told him.

"What did you major in?" another boy, Jeremy, asked.

Another one asked, "Where do you live?"

The questions kept coming at her until an older woman walked through the door. She had light brown hair with strands of gray showing through the pageboy-style cut. "Hey, kids, you don't want to scare off Sam's new waitress, do you?"

Several heads turned. "Hello, Mrs. Hunter," the teenagers called out in unison.

"Hello, kids," she greeted them. "Now, go dance or I'll send you over to the school and have you clean up my classroom to burn off all your energy."

With a groan, the kids dispersed, leaving Tori alone with the woman.

She extended her hand. "Hello, I'm Betty Hunter, better known as Nate, Shane and Emily's mother, or Mrs. H, the fourth-grade teacher."

Tori shook her hand. "Tori Sheridan. Pleased to meet you." The slender woman was beautiful and in no way looked old enough to be Nate's mother.

The music changed and Otis Redding's "Sitting on the Dock of the Bay" filled the room.

"I think everyone in town knows who you are," Mrs. Hunter said. "It's one of the not-so-great things about small towns. Everyone knows everybody's business." Her smile brightened. "I hope you can put up with us and stay awhile."

Tori saw the woman's questioning gaze. "Since my car is out of commission, it looks like that's going to happen. And everyone has been so nice and helpful. I'm especially grateful to your son."

"It's nice to know that I raised him right."

"May I get you something?"

"An iced tea, please."

Tori scooped ice into a tall glass, then filled it from the pitcher of tea. After adding a lemon wedge, she returned to the counter. Mrs. Hunter turned away from the kids dancing to the Righteous Brothers' "Unchained Melody" with a dreamy look in her dark brown eyes. "Sorry, I'd drifted back a few decades. My husband and I loved to dance." She sighed. "That was a long time ago."

Tori was amazed at the play of emotions across Betty Hunter's face. Even after ten years she still loved her husband. "Seems a new generation is keeping the era alive," Tori said.

"And Sam won't let them forget." Mrs. Hunter laughed. "I think he's taught all the boys how to dance. He's not bad, either. Pretty light on his feet for a big guy, and he makes the best burgers around. And this is a place where their parents let them come to hang out."

"It's a great place."

"Maybe you won't say that after you've heard Elvis sing 'Love Me Tender' a hundred times."

Right now Tori didn't want to be anywhere else. "Did you let your children come here?"

Her smile faded. "We lived outside of town back then." There was a long pause and she brightened once again. "I heard you own a classic Corvette."

Tori nodded. "That doesn't have a rear end."

"All I know is Ernie has never had so many visitors in his shop."

"I never realized that I would cause so much commotion."

"It's not every day that we get a visitor in Haven—population, 3,772 residents. We have one school, one post office, three churches and two beauty salons. But we're growing, with the new electronics plant outside of town and the new housing development."

Tori smiled. "And I hear that your younger son, Shane, is the builder. You must be proud of your children."

"I am, including my daughter, Emily. She's away at college in Tempe." Betty took another drink of her tea. "What about you, Tori? Do you have family?"

Before Tori could answer, the café door opened and Nate walked in. He looked around and waved at several of the kids, then turned his attention to the counter. He smiled, then sat down next to his mother. Tori could see the family resemblance, except for Nate's coloring, which he must have gotten from his father. But his silvery green eyes were his mother's.

"Hey, Mom, what are you up to?"

"Just visiting with Tori. Thought it was time I came

by and welcomed her to town and asked her to come to a barbecue on Saturday. I think I'll invite Sam, too." She stood and headed back to the kitchen before anyone could respond.

Nate decided his mother was cooking up something besides her famously delicious barbecue chicken.

"Nate, really, I don't need to come," Tori broke in.

"Are you kidding? My mother loves an excuse to have a party. School is out on Friday and she's getting geared up for the summer."

Nate knew he should stay away from Tori Sheridan. He needed to concentrate on the auction, not get involved with this woman—a woman who was just passing through town. Soon she'd go back to her life, and his was planned out to get back the Double H.

Besides, he seriously doubted that she was the type of woman who would want to live in a one-hundred-year-old ranch house. But then he didn't think she would last as a waitress at the café, either. So if she was going to be in town for a few weeks why not enjoy her company?

"I could come by and pick you up Saturday," he suggested. Where did that come from? "It's not a date or anything... I mean I—uh, don't expect you to think that."

Her cheeks reddened. "Of course. And I appreciate your offer."

He nodded. "Okay. I'll be by at about six."

She smiled and his body stirred. "That sounds fine."

He stood, feeling about as awkward as he imagined Matt Hillenbrand had this morning. Damn, it had been too long since he'd gone out on a date. But this wasn't a date, he reminded himself. "I'll see you Saturday then." Somehow he got out the door before he made a complete fool of himself.

Chapter Four

Saturday afternoon, Nate walked up the wooden staircase to Tori's apartment. He smiled when he saw a small potted plant placed on the landing along with a colorful welcome mat. He also realized he was a little breathless. He told himself it was the climb and not the fact he was anxious to see Tori that had taken his breath away. He paused and leaned against the railing.

He had been looking forward to spending the evening with her. Maybe more than he should. This wasn't the time to think about romancing a woman. Not yet. Not until he had the Double H back and a place he could call home.

For so long his focus had been on his family responsibilities. Most of the women he'd dated over the years had gotten tired of putting up with the attention he gave to his mother and siblings. Nate had never minded because his family was important to him. He just wished that he'd discovered their importance sooner. Then maybe he would have had more time with his father.

He shook away the past regrets, vowing that he wasn't going to make that mistake again.

Tori probably wouldn't be in Haven long enough for it to matter, Nate thought to himself as he walked to her door. She'd be headed back to San Francisco soon, but why not enjoy each other's company?

He knocked on the weathered door, and within a heartbeat it opened and Tori stood there in a pair of white shorts and a hot-pink shirt. Her blond hair lay in soft waves around her shoulders. Once again he couldn't seem to draw enough air into his lungs.

She tossed him one of her easy smiles. "Hello, Nate."

He cleared his throat. "Hi," he said. "You ready?"

"Just give me one more minute." She stepped aside so he could come into the room.

Nate hadn't been here since the day he helped her clean up. He noticed that a few things had been added. There were small plants scattered around and two colorful place mats covered the chipped counter. The changes weren't expensive, but he'd learned from his mother that women liked to add their own touches in decorating their homes.

"The place looks nice."

She shrugged. "I just found a few things that made it seem more…homey."

He glanced at the bed. A thin blue bedspread covered the double mattress and he wondered if she stayed cool enough at night. He glanced back at her and her gaze met his. "How are you sleeping?"

"Soundly," she said. "Working at the café has its advantages. I get plenty of exercise and I can probably eat anything these days and not have to worry about my weight."

He couldn't resist looking over her trim yet curvy body. She was perfect. "Good, because Mom is a great cook. Speaking of which, we better get going before my brother eats everything."

"I'm ready." She picked up her purse and a small African violet plant. She noticed his interest. "I heard from Sam that your mother likes violets."

Nate swallowed the dryness in his throat as he stared at his mom's favorite flower. The thoughtful gesture drew him even more to this woman. No doubt Betty Hunter would think Tori was a keeper, too. Too bad she wasn't going to stay in Haven.

Tori loved the quiet, tree-lined street in the older neighborhood where the Hunters lived. This area looked more like the Midwest than southwest Arizona.

Nate pulled into the driveway of the two-story, cream-colored clapboard house with the burgundy shutters. The lawn was lush and green, and flower boxes were filled with a rainbow of colorful spring annuals.

"Your home is lovely," she remarked.

"It's my mother's place. I live over the garage."

Tori wasn't surprised by Nate's admission. She'd already learned about the sheriff's situation from Sam.

Nate climbed out of the truck and walked around to help her down. She put her purse strap over her shoulder and reached back into the cab for the plant.

"As you can see my mother has quite a green thumb." His large hand went to the small of her back, and she immediately recalled when he'd held her against him to discourage Matt Hillenbrand. This seemed different. He didn't have to touch her, nor did she have to enjoy it so much. Then she made a mistake and glanced up at him and found him looking at her with those incredible gray eyes. Her legs seemed to lose their strength and her walking slowed, but not her heart rate. This was bad. The last thing she needed was to develop feelings for the good-looking sheriff. Not when her heart had been torn apart just a week ago. She was in a weakened condition, but that didn't seem to matter to her out-of-control libido. Her gaze moved to his mouth as she wondered what it would feel like to kiss him.

The sound of laughter drew her attention back to her surroundings. "I guess the party has already started," Nate said and guided her along the driveway to where voices were coming from the backyard.

He opened a high wooden gate. The backyard was as lovely as the front, a lush green lawn lined with multicolored roses climbing over trellises. A rough wood arbor covered a slate patio.

"It's about time you got here." A tall well-built man who looked remarkably like Nate came toward them. This was no doubt the younger brother, Shane. Like Nate, he was dressed in a T-shirt, jeans and athletic shoes. His dark hair was a lot longer, but it worked for him. He studied her with those same deep-set eyes and offered her a charming smile. Tori didn't miss the interested look he gave her, a rather exaggerated once-over, making Tori smile.

"Now I can see why you wanted to keep this one all to yourself." Nate's brother reached out and took her hand in his. "Hi, I'm Shane, the smarter and handsomer brother. Want to ditch this old guy and run off with me?"

With a nervous laugh, Tori shook his hand. "I'm sorry, Shane, I always go home with the guy that brought me." Suddenly, realizing what her words suggested, she couldn't help but blush.

Something flickered in Shane's eyes, then he shrugged. "Can't blame a guy for trying."

"Go find your own woman." Nate's possessive grip tightened around Tori's waist. "If you promise to behave, I'll introduce you properly. Tori Sheridan, this is my brother, Shane. Shane, this is Tori."

"It's a pleasure to meet you, Tori Sheridan."

"Hello, Shane." She fought to control her nervous laughter.

"I hear you're working for Sam. I guess I'll have to stop by for a visit." He leaned forward. "I don't give up easily."

"You'd better," Nate said. "Remember, I'm the law around here."

Shane grinned. "So that's how it is?" The two men stared at one another until they were interrupted by a woman's voice.

"Shane Michael Hunter," Betty Hunter said. "You be nice."

Their mother appeared next to her sons. "Tori, I'm glad you could make it."

"Thank you for inviting me." She handed Betty the plant.

"Oh, this is lovely. Thank you."

A younger and taller version of Betty appeared beside her. The girl was pretty with dark brown hair and rich blue eyes that resembled Shane's. This had to be Emily.

Nate did the introductions. "Tori, you've already met my mother and Shane. This is my sister, Emily. Emily, this is Tori Sheridan."

Emily offered her hand. "Nice to meet you, Tori."

"The same to you. How do you keep these two guys in line?"

"It isn't easy, but now that you're here, we women finally have them outnumbered."

"Don't get too cocky. We've got Sam coming," Nate said.

Betty gave a laugh. "He's a pussycat." She motioned everyone to the patio table. Six places were set with colorful yellow plates. Nate held back and whispered in

Tori's ear. "Mom only says that because Sam's been crazy about her for years."

"Really?"

He nodded. "I think everyone knows it except Sam and Mom." Tori let Nate take her hand and tug her to the table. Before he took a seat, he asked, "How about something to drink? Beer? Wine? Soda?"

Tori knew she should keep her wits about her, but this was her first night out after a hard but satisfying week of work. "A cold beer sounds good."

"My kind of girl." Nate winked at her and her pulse shot off. In no time he returned with a bottle of beer and a glass. He poured half the contents into the glass then handed it to her.

Their fingers brushed and she felt a scorching heat, but it wasn't from the Arizona sun. "Thank you."

"You're welcome," he said, then sat down next to her. Their gazes held until Emily's voice broke the spell.

Tori turned in her direction. "Excuse me. What did you say?"

"I asked if you plan to stay in Haven for long?"

"Honestly, I hadn't even planned to stop at all, but, as everyone knows, my car broke down." She found she was a little embarrassed about her circumstances, but no one else seemed to be. "I was stranded on the highway when Nate found me."

"Nate to the rescue," Shane cheered from across the table.

Tori knew she had a lot to thank the sheriff for. "Well,

I'm grateful. He talked Sam into giving me a job to help pay for the repairs on my car—and a place to stay."

"And you're the best waitress I've had in a long time."

Everyone turned to see the burly man come though the gate.

"Sam," Betty called as she got up to greet him. "I'm glad you could make it." She took him by the arm and brought him to the table. "Sit down and relax."

He handed her a white paper sack. "I brought some coleslaw."

Betty smiled and hugged him. "Oh, my favorite."

Tori would have sworn Sam was blushing. So her boss did have a thing for Betty Hunter.

"Good, now I can get the steaks started." Nate got up, walked to the large aluminum grill and opened the lid. "I'll get the fire going."

"Is there anything I can do to help?" Tori called.

Three men gave her a puzzled look. Had she said something wrong?

"No, we're in charge tonight," Nate said.

Emily leaned close and whispered, "It's a guy thing. Cooking outside. Like we couldn't turn on a gas grill and throw on some meat?"

Tori wouldn't know. Her father had never cooked on a grill. In fact, she'd never known him to cook at all. Had J.C. or Jed ever been in a kitchen?

She looked at Nate. Obviously Betty had taught her sons to cook and it hadn't done anything to diminish their manhood. She watched as Sam and Shane joined

Nate at the grill. The trio stood together talking, sharing news of the day, a joke or a story. Their laughter rang out, and it was contagious.

Suddenly Nate glanced at her. He gave her a sexy wink, causing a funny stirring in her stomach.

Oh, no, Nate Hunter didn't need any help at all in that department.

An hour later, Nate realized he had made it through the meal without being embarrassed by his family. Not too many questions about the woman he'd brought to dinner, or about his plans, or how serious he was about Tori Sheridan.

And he'd enjoyed the time spent with Tori. Maybe too much. She'd fitted in so easily. He could see by the pleased look on his mother's face that she liked Tori. So did Shane. Of course, since Tori was a pretty woman, that was a given. Even his toughest critic, his baby sister, seemed to get along with the newest town resident.

So why was he worried? A lot of reasons. He was afraid that he couldn't keep things with Tori just casual. From the first moment he'd seen her, he'd been attracted to her. More so since she'd shown him her determination and grit. But what would happen when her debts were paid? Was she going to drive off into the sunset in her classic Corvette? Could he stop her?

No, she would leave…unless she found a reason to stay. Did he want to be that reason? He shook away the thought. Hell, he didn't even know if she had someone waiting for her.

Just then he saw his mother take Tori into the house. Oh, boy. Hard telling what she was up to. She was probably dragging out a photo album, or worse, his football trophies. He made a move to follow them when he felt Sam's hand on his arm.

"Let your mother have some time with Tori."

"So she can grill her?"

Sam frowned. "Betty isn't going to do anything to embarrass you. She just wants to know what kind of woman has gotten her son's attention."

Nate blew out a breath. "How long is this going to take?"

Sam nodded at Nate's full beer bottle. "Just relax and enjoy your drink."

As if he could. He hadn't been able to relax since Tori Sheridan had arrived in town.

Betty showed Tori into the living room. Tori took in the beautiful antique sideboard, probably handed down through the family.

The room was decorated in warm earth tones. Thriving potted plants lined the ledge of the huge picture window that was framed with a rich burgundy valance and eggshell-colored sheers. Gleaming hardwood floors were partly covered by a taupe rug. A floral-print sofa faced the brick fireplace where family photos were arranged along the oak mantel.

This was nothing like her father's dark mansion. There were no Picassos on the walls, no crystal chandeliers or gold brocade drapes framing the million-dollar view from the hill.

The Hunter house was a real family home. She had felt it the second she walked in.

"Betty, your home is lovely," Tori said as she turned around to gaze at the carved oak banister leading to the second floor.

"Thank you." Betty sighed. "Believe me, it wasn't like this when we bought it. Saying the place needed work is an understatement. But Nate and Shane spent a lot of their spare time renovating it."

"It's nice that you have such talented sons." Tori walked to a curio cabinet, noticing the small wooden sculptures inside. Curious, she leaned closer. She was mesmerized by a carved eagle perched on a branch, his wings spread ready to take flight. Her attention moved to another shelf where there was a wolf chiseled out of a darker wood. Next to it was a horse, a stallion rearing up on his hind legs. The fine, delicate lines in the wood gave each sculpture a unique identity and power.

"They're beautiful, aren't they?" Betty asked as she came to stand by Tori.

"Oh, yes." Tori found she couldn't take her eyes off the sculptures. "Is the artist local?"

"Very local. In fact, he lives over the garage."

Then the older woman smiled as the truth dawned on Tori. "Nate? Nate carved these?"

Betty nodded, opened the cabinet, took out the wolf and handed it to Tori. "His grandfather Nathan taught Nate to whittle when he was only six. I was scared to death seeing my child with a knife in his small hand. But Nate learned quickly and his grandfather was always there to guide him."

Tori caressed the exquisite piece. "This is a lot more than just whittling."

"So, I'm not the only one who thinks he has talent."

Tori had been to art galleries all over the world. "Oh, my, no. The detail is incredible. Each character seems to come alive. Has he approached any galleries?"

Betty shook her head. "He says he just makes them for friends and family. He doesn't want it to be a job."

Tori glanced in the cabinet and counted eight pieces. "How many years has he been doing this?"

"Consistently over the past ten years or so. Ever since his injury when he returned home from college."

Just then Nate walked into the room. "Looks like I'm just in time to rescue you from my bragging mother."

"She has every reason to brag. These are beautiful."

"Thank you," he acknowledged, no doubt embarrassed. "It's a hobby, nothing more. It relaxes me." His expression told her that he didn't want to linger on the subject. "Hey, how do you ladies feel about playing a little poker?"

It was after nine o'clock. Tori should ask to go home. She knew that she should end the evening. She had to work early in the morning and she didn't need to get any cozier in Nate's life.

But there was an irresistible glint in his eyes. "Of course, if you're afraid we'll beat you ladies…"

Tori had learned to play poker when she was a kid. Her father made sure of it. J.C. had insisted she needed the bluffing skills for business.

"I guess I can stay awhile longer," she agreed. If only to wipe that smile off the sheriff's face. "I hope you don't play for too much money."

"Nah, Mom only allows penny poker."

"Okay, but you're going to have to help me," Tori said as she glanced over her shoulder and winked at Betty, then followed Nate outside.

For the next hour they played five-card stud with jacks or better to open. Nate thought himself a pretty good judge of people, but Tori had him totally confused. Then he finally figured it out.

Ms. Sheridan was a card shark.

She'd been fooling everyone, acting as if she knew nothing about poker, losing hand after hand until the tide slowly began to change in her favor. She acted surprised when she finally won a hand. Then it was her turn to shuffle and suddenly her small hands knew expertly how to handle the cards. The next five hands she won, and now she was about to clean out Sam and Shane in one fell swoop.

Shane grinned and eyed the pile of chips in the center of the table, then laid out his cards. Two pair, jacks over sixes. He tipped his chair back and waited.

"Darn. That beats my two queens," Sam said as he tossed in his cards. All eyes turned to the only player left.

"What've you got, Tori?" asked Emily, who'd run out of money thirty minutes ago. Betty was penniless, too. Nate decided Tori had gotten him enough times and just enjoyed watching her play the game.

Ms. Card Shark Sheridan blew out a long breath. "I'm not sure if I can beat the queens."

"We're not falling for that innocent look anymore," Sam said. "Just show us your hand."

One by one she laid out her cards. First came a two, a five and a ten, a jack, lastly a king. Looked like junk, except they were all the same suit. Diamonds. Collective male groans erupted as the ladies cheered and Tori gathered up her winnings. Nate scooted his chair back and stood.

"Why do you even bother to work?" Shane asked. "You should just play poker."

"I'm not that good. You guys are just too easy to read."

The men groaned again and the ladies exchanged high fives.

Nate couldn't help but smile at Tori's savvy—among other things. "I think it's time I got Tori home." He realized he was tired of sharing her and wanted some alone time. He wasn't going to fight the attraction any longer.

"Maybe she isn't ready to go," Shane complained.

Nate glanced at Tori. She seemed surprised at his request, but when his eyes held hers the heat between them intensified. He wanted to hold her in his arms, kiss her until he couldn't think anymore. Did she want the same?

"How about it, Tori? You ready to go?"

She nodded as she checked her watch. "Yes. I should leave. I need to get to bed." Her face reddened. "I mean… I have to get up for the early shift at the café."

She busied herself gathering up her coins, then stopped. "Why don't I just leave this? For when we play again."

"Listen," Shane proclaimed. "I'll count it up for you and bring your winnings by the café."

Nate didn't like his brother's suggestion and took Tori's hand. "Whatever. Now, I need to get Tori home."

Tori didn't pull away. "Thank you, Betty, for the wonderful evening. Nice to meet you, Shane, Emily," she said, and Nate tugged her toward the gate.

When they reached his truck, he opened the door and helped her in. "Buckle up," he told her, then went around to the other side, still a little miffed over his brother's obvious interest in his date. So what? Shane flirted with every female. Besides, Tori Sheridan wasn't his girl—woman—or whatever. And he needed to remember that.

Nate started the engine and backed out of the driveway. The trip back to the café only took about ten minutes, but the silence between them made it seem like forever. Finally he pulled up in the dark alley and parked, but didn't get out.

"Is something wrong?" Tori finally asked. "I mean, are you upset because of the poker?"

"No, it wasn't the game," he told her, inhaling her fresh scent.

He turned to her. The streetlight shining through the windshield causing a halo around her blond hair. Her eyes were wide and questioning. His gaze moved to her mouth as she nibbled nervously on her lower lip. Desire hit him in the gut as he struggled to pull air into his lungs.

Keep things light. Fat chance, he thought as he suddenly realized how much he wanted Tori. Just get your butt out of the truck, walk her upstairs and say good-night.

She fidgeted in the uncomfortable silence. "Well… I want to thank you for taking me tonight. Your family is wonderful. You should be grateful you have them. Thanks again." She popped open her seat belt and reached for the door handle.

Nate's resistance was gone, along with any common sense. He released his seat belt, then reached for her. She gasped in surprise as he pulled her across to his side of the cab and into his arms. He saw the startled look on her face. He was definitely out of his mind, but she was the one causing his irrational behavior.

His hand stroked her soft cheek. She was so beautiful. "If you don't want this, now is the time to say something."

For what seemed like an eternity, she was quiet, then her hands went to his chest and she leaned toward him. He hesitated only a second before his mouth captured hers.

Chapter Five

Excitement raced through Tori's veins. All the feelings she'd thought dead suddenly awakened as Nate's skilled mouth moved over hers, teasing, tasting, taking and giving pleasure. An urgent need spiraled through her as never before when his hands dug into her hair and he deepened the kiss. Oh, and she was a willing participant. She slid her arms around his neck and she pressed herself into his solid body.

She was close to surrendering, to forgetting everything but this man, to being lost in the here and now. But she still couldn't hide from the lingering pain of Jed's betrayal. Suddenly tears filled her eyes, and with the last of her strength, she pulled away.

Tori gasped. "I can't do this." And before Nate could

respond, she slid out of the truck. She made it to the top of the steps before he caught up with her.

"Tori, please. At least tell me what I did wrong."

She paused at the door, but, not wanting him to see her tears, she wouldn't look at him.

"You didn't do anything. I shouldn't have let you kiss me."

She heard his long sigh. "I guess I didn't give you much choice. I'm sorry I rushed you."

This time she did turn around. "No, you gave me every opportunity to stop things." She glanced away, unable to handle the raw look in his eyes. It would be so easy to lean on him. "I'm just not ready for this."

He took a step closer. "I know you were involved with someone else."

"No!" she denied too quickly. "Not anymore." It was hard to believe that two weeks ago she was about to marry Jed. Now, she was kissing another man. "I broke it off."

Silently, he stepped closer, but instead of crowding her, he leaned back against the railing, his large body silhouetted by the moonlight. "I take it your ex was the reason you left San Francisco."

She hesitated then finally nodded.

"Are you worried he's following you?"

"Oh, no." She doubted Jed even missed her, but her father was a different story. J.C. didn't like to be crossed. "I left him a message and sent back his ring…" Good Lord, she was telling Nate far too much. "Let's just say it was a mistake." Almost the biggest in my life. The biggest mistake was to believe that her father had ever loved her, ever cared about her happiness.

"The man was a fool to let you walk away."

Nate's baritone voice was like a warm caress. She raised her gaze to his. To those beautiful, silvery eyes, his sexy mouth. A shiver raced along her spine as she remembered how just moments ago he'd held her in his arms and kissed her so thoroughly. She quickly stopped her wayward thoughts, recalling her vow to be independent. Now was not the time to get involved with another man.

"Maybe I was to blame, too. Sometimes we overlook a lot of things because we want a home and a family so badly. We're willing to accept a trade-off." She hated to admit it, but that was so true.

"Oh, Tori. You deserve so much more. You don't need to settle for anything less than it all." Nate took her hand, raised it to his lips and placed a kiss against her fingers. She felt the jolt all the way up her arm, saw the desire in his eyes. "I'm going to say good-night now, before I get into more trouble," he whispered. With a squeeze of her hand, he released her, then walked down the stairs.

Tori fought to keep from calling him back and asking him to stay with her, to ease her loneliness.

Nate glanced up one last time before he climbed into the truck. When he didn't leave, she realized he was waiting for her to go inside. She hurriedly unlocked the door and went into the apartment. When she heard the truck engine come to life, she sank back against the door.

"You're in big trouble, Victoria Ann. You don't need another man in your already messed-up life." She closed her eyes and relived Nate's kiss, the gentleness of his touch against her skin. Her body immediately came to life, her breathing grew labored, her pulse began to race. What would it be like if she hadn't sent the good-looking sheriff home tonight? She'd never been promiscuous. Of course, she hadn't had much experience with men since she'd had few beaus before Jed. She'd always felt she wasn't pretty enough, flirty enough. Tori had concentrated on school and later on her career. Thinking back, she wondered how much J.C. had had to do with her lack of confidence.

But her father wasn't around now.

Her thoughts turned back to Nate. It was as if her body had suddenly been awakened by his touch. As much as she tried to deny it, she wanted Nate Hunter. What would it be like to make love with him? She blew out a long breath.

That was a fantasy she couldn't let come true.

The next morning came too soon for Nate, especially after his restless night. When he couldn't sleep he'd gotten up and gone into his workshop, hoping that carving a piece of mesquite would clear his head. It hadn't worked. In fact, it hadn't even come close to driving Tori from his head. Not when their kiss replayed over and over again during the long, lonely night. At least he'd come to the realization that one taste of her could never be enough.

He managed to hold out until noon before he made an appearance at the café. He'd be happy now if he could just keep from making a fool out of himself. After greeting several of Sam's customers, he took his usual place at the counter and fought to keep from searching the room for Tori.

When laughter broke out in the far booth, he gave up and twisted around on the bar stool to see her. She was dressed in her usual short-skirted uniform. Her blond hair was up off her long neck in a ponytail, but a few of her wild curls had escaped their neat confines. She was busy talking to the group of men seated in the booth. He didn't know any of them, except for one. Shane. And he was holding Tori's attention…along with her hand.

Nate's back straightened. His younger brother had always told him that he didn't have time for a lunch break away from the construction site; however, he seemed to have plenty of time today.

Nate got up and walked across the room to the happy group in time to hear Shane say, "Hey, Tori, when are you going to shuck this job and run away with me?"

"As soon as I believe you're serious," she tossed back and the group broke into laughter.

"How can she take you seriously when you've used that same line on every woman in town?" Nate interrupted as he approached the table.

Tori turned immediately and her cheeks reddened.

"Oh, Nate." She fidgeted with the dishes in her hands. "I didn't see you come in."

His gaze shifted to his brother. "I'm sure Shane was demanding all your attention. He was like that as a kid, too. Always doing some silly stunt to get people to notice him."

Shane lost his grin. "I had to keep up with my big brother."

"Well, you're all grown up and running a company now. And hey, I thought you were too busy to stop for lunch."

Shane glanced at Tori. "I guess I just found a good reason to take a break."

"Speaking of which," Tori interrupted them, "I need to help my other customers." She turned and hurried off. Every guy at the table watched her hips sway as she walked away.

One of the workers spoke up. "Man, she's the hottest thing I've seen in this town since I've been here."

Nate didn't like the guy's leer. "And the last thing Tori needs is for you guys to harass her."

"I didn't know Tori asked you to be her keeper," Shane remarked.

"Someone has to protect her from you yahoos."

Shane came to his feet. "What's the matter, bro, you afraid of the competition?"

"This isn't a competition," Nate insisted, knowing he was lying. "I just said she didn't need a hassle right now."

Before Shane could defend himself Nate heard his name called out. He saw Sam standing in the kitchen pass-through window. "Could you come back here a minute?"

Nate gave his brother one last warning look. "Just don't be bugging her all the time," he said, then went back to see Sam. "What's up, Sam?"

"Not much." The older guy shrugged as he placed several hamburger patties on the grill. It immediately began to sizzle. He opened half a dozen buns along the counter and squirted on the mayonnaise, then layered them with tomatoes and pickles. "I just thought I'd save myself some trouble." He wiped his hands on his apron and picked up the spatula.

"What are you talking about?" Nate asked.

"You and Shane are acting like a couple of bulls fighting over a heifer."

"I wasn't doing that." Was he?

"I know you think Tori needs your help, but she's more than capable of handling things." He smiled. "I've watched her in action. Besides, Shane hits on all females, young or old."

"And why should I care who talks to Tori?"

Sam gave a mock scowl. "Because you're so easy to read. Shane knows you're interested in Tori so he's flirting with her to bug you."

"Damn, this isn't high school."

"Then stop acting like it is," Sam said.

Nate rubbed his hands over his face. "I don't need this. I have too many things to worry about. And I sure don't need Tori Sheridan to add to the list."

"Love doesn't always arrive at a convenient time in your life. But if she's the one, don't be foolish enough to let her slip away."

Love! Nate didn't want to hear any more. He didn't have time. "I've got to get out of here." Instead of going through the café, he marched out the back door leading to the alley.

From now on he was going to stay far away from the Good Time Café and Tori Sheridan.

Could her day get any worse?

At two o'clock Tori approached a table of dirty dishes and began clearing up the mess.

Her troubles had started when she'd overslept this morning. She'd only had ten minutes to get into her uniform and to work. Not getting much sleep last night had been her fault. She never should have let Nate kiss her. The man had stirred up too many feelings, and thoughts of him had distracted her all day. And things just got worse when he came in, looking too good to ignore. Did the man realize the effect he had on every female in town?

Suddenly the glasses she was gathering clinked together and one toppled over onto the floor, shattering into tiny pieces.

"Why don't you sit down before I go broke," Sam said as he walked across the empty café with a small hand broom and dustpan.

"Oh, Sam, I'm sorry. I'll pay for everything I broke today. Just take it out of my check."

The big guy smiled and he brushed the broken glass into the pan. "The hell with the dishes. Considering the circus you've had to put up with today, I'd say you did good."

"What are you talking about?"

"You seem to be attracting a lot of male customers."

"Oh, gosh, do you think I'm being too friendly?"

"No, I think you're being too nice. I'd say a lot of that construction crew need to learn some manners. And then you have the Hunter boys pushing at each other to get to you."

Tori sank into the nearest chair. "I swear, Sam, I never—" She hadn't meant to cause problems between brothers.

"I know. Just don't take Shane's flirting seriously. He loves all women. But he does have Nate a little riled." Sam shook his head. "Haven't seen that in a long time."

"The last thing I want is to cause any trouble. Everyone has been so nice."

"I know. But Nate likes you." Sam's soft hazel eyes met hers. "And I think you care about him, too." He raised a hand. "Now, I'm not saying that anything's got to come of it. I just want you to know that you couldn't do any better than Nate Hunter."

Before Tori could say anything, he picked up a stack of dishes. "Now, we better get this place cleaned up before the schoolkids get here."

Sam walked to the counter and Tori worked to slow her pulse. No, she didn't want Nate to care about her. As soon as she got enough money together to pay for her car repairs, she was leaving town. She had too many other things to deal with. Finding a permanent place to live, a job. Her life was a mess. A man would only complicate things more.

"Thank you, Sheriff Nate," the young students sang out in unison the following Monday morning.

"You're very welcome, boys and girls," Nate said as he walked to the door of his mother's classroom.

It was his day off, but when Mom had asked for his help he hadn't hesitated.

Two years ago, Betty Hunter had convinced the school board to let her begin a summer program to help kids who had trouble in certain subjects, like math and reading. Then she'd manned the program with volunteers: parents, retired people and professionals in the community.

The program had been a success, so much so that she'd started plans to do the same for the high school. The curriculum would consist of practical classes like financial planning, preparing for college and other career choices. She'd even talked to Shane about a carpentry apprenticeship program.

His mother was a firm believer that the hard work involved would pay off when these young people became good, productive Haven citizens.

"I can't thank you enough for coming today," she said as she met him just outside her classroom.

"No problem. It's my day off." He shrugged. "I'm just headed out to the Double H."

She smiled. "Are you doing the estimates today?"

Nate nodded. He knew he shouldn't jump the gun. The place wasn't even his…yet. But he wanted the Double H so badly he could taste it. "Shane's going to meet me later to look at the damage to the barn."

His mother glanced over her shoulder into her classroom to see if the kids were working, then turned back to him. "It's definitely a solid structure. Your Grandpa Nate built it. But you should only buy the ranch because you want it. Not because you feel it's expected of you."

"I know what I want, Mom. The Double H."

She smiled. "Then maybe you should concentrate on finding someone special and having a family."

He sighed. She would never give up. "Maybe," he said and started to leave when his mom stopped him.

"One more favor, son. Could you take this box of books over to the library for me?"

"Sure." He picked up the box and started down the hall toward the same library room he'd gone to as a kid. He glanced around at the familiar surroundings, the rows of shelves filled with books, and the desk where Mrs. Jorgen used to sit and hush everyone. He set the box on the return book cart and his attention went to a round table where a blond woman was listening to one of the kids read. Tori Sheridan raised her head and her rich brown eyes met his. It only took one minute to realize that his own mother had set him up.

Tori could barely speak the words as her throat suddenly went dry. She tried not to be distracted by Nate's presence, but she was. Why now? Why after a week did he have to show up here?

All at once the bell rang and she jumped. The group of seven- and eight-year-old children stood, tossed quick thank-yous and hurried toward the exit. Some slowed and greeted Nate on their way out. He smiled at them, ruffled the hair of a couple of the boys. She enjoyed watching the easy way he had with kids. And it was obvious they respected him. It was so refreshing when you came from a place where a lot of people thought authority was the enemy. That was not the case in Haven. Not with Sheriff Nate.

Once the room emptied, he turned to her with those light gray eyes. As hard as she tried she couldn't slow her racing pulse. Just his presence seemed to overwhelm her. His fitted khaki uniform emphasized his broad shoulders and narrow hips. A wide black leather belt held his holstered sidearm, but the gun didn't seem as threatening as the man himself. His gait was slow and deliberate as he came across the room. His gaze never wavered from hers.

"Looks like my mother got you involved in her program, too."

She tried to busy her shaky hands by gathering up the books. "I was glad to help. It's so important to get the kids off to a good start. I'm working in the reading program." She looked at him. Big mistake. She lost her breath again, hoping it was caused by the dry Arizona air. "Why are you here?"

"Oh, I come in several times a year and talk about

safety to the younger kids. To the older ones, it's about drinking and driving, or a career in law enforcement."

She had no doubt that he could give an interesting talk. "Can you take the time when you're on duty?"

"It's my day off."

"Mine, too."

They stood there for what seemed like an eternity. Tori had never been good at small talk. It was one of the things her father had often reprimanded her about. J.C. had told her she needed to be able to hold her own in any conversation. Once she had been able to talk freely with Nate, but then he'd kissed her. And worse, she'd kissed him back. Ever since then she had been totally tongue-tied around him.

He finally spoke. "Well, I guess I'd better get going. And I'm sure you have things to do. Can I give you a lift?"

"No, I'm fine. What's nice about this town is just about everything is within walking distance."

Tori believed he'd been avoiding her for the past week. Of course, she'd basically told him to leave her alone and that she couldn't get involved with him. So why did she feel he was rejecting her? "I need to stop by Ernie's garage. I want to make a payment toward my car repairs."

"I'm sure he'll appreciate that," Nate said and they both started out of the room. "Perhaps I'll stop by Ernie's sometime, too, seeing as how I will have the pleasure of driving your little beauty once it's fixed." He smiled as they continued down the hall and out of the building.

Nate paused at the curb. "Well, I guess I'll go," he said again, but stayed where he was.

Tori decided she had to be smart and began to back away. "Have a nice day off." She checked traffic, then stepped off the curb.

"Tori, wait."

She stopped and turned around.

"Are you busy after you go to Ernie's? I mean, do you have plans for this afternoon?"

Lie. You don't need to spend any more time with him. You've already started to have feelings for the man. Not heeding her own warning, she answered, "No, just cleaning the apartment."

He tossed her that sexy grin and she nearly moaned out loud. "On a beautiful day like this you're going to be inside? I have a better idea. How about taking a ride in the country with me?"

Chapter Six

An hour later, Nate was headed to the Double H Ranch with a smile on his face and Tori seated next to him. He'd decided he could handle spending a little time with her. He just had to keep things light. She'd be leaving in a few weeks, so why not enjoy each other's company and this nice day? Sure, that was easy. All he had to do was ignore the way she filled out a pair of shorts, or how the rosy-colored blouse she was wearing draped so perfectly over her curves.

Nate turned off the highway onto the dirt-and-gravel road. He immediately slowed as he worked to maneuver around the numerous potholes caused by bad weather and neglect.

"Sorry," he said and glanced across the seat to see

Tori grab the safety handle as the truck bounced down the road.

"Just where is this place you're taking me?"

"About a quarter mile up the road. Sorry about the rough ride."

She smiled at him. "The scenery is worth it."

Nate glanced out the windshield at the cactus and mesquite scattered across the open range. Off in the distance they could see the Dos Cabezas Mountains. The sun-bleached terra-cotta rock formations were dotted with green from the trees and shrubs, a magnificent contrast against the rich blue desert sky.

"I guess being raised here I've taken it for granted."

"Oh, I never would," she said. "I grew up in the city, with noise and traffic. Not that San Francisco isn't beautiful, but this takes your breath away."

"I'm glad you like the scenery, because I can't say much for the rest of the place." Although right now, he'd give almost anything to have the run-down ranch back, he thought.

Tori was quiet as they drove under the leaning wrought-iron sign. She couldn't make out the words, but she knew from Sam that this must be the place that had once been the Hunter family ranch. She looked along the road at the broken-down fences encircling a pasture with knee-high weeds. Then they drove past a huge faded red barn and outbuildings that had once been white.

Nate pulled into a circular driveway and stopped in

front of a two-story wooden house. It, too, had been shamefully neglected. The shiplap siding was a washed-out yellow and many of the boards were rotted. The windows were broken and the shutters hung cockeyed. The large porch was missing the hand railing and several of the posts were gone.

"Home sweet home," he said.

She glanced sideways at Nate. "This is yours?"

"It had been in the Hunter family for over a hundred years. Then my dad died and we lost the place."

Tori could hear the sadness in his voice. "I'm sorry."

He blew out a breath. "It comes up for auction the middle of July. I aim to get it back. I'm hoping to be the only one who will want it."

"So you're going to be a rancher."

He nodded. "It's in my blood. But I can only afford to ranch part-time. It's going to take a lot of money and work to get this place back in shape."

Her hand went to the door handle. "May I look around?" she asked.

"Just don't go running off too far." He glanced down at her bare legs and tennis shoes. "I wouldn't want you disturbing any varmints."

She paused. "How big are these varmints?"

He puffed out his chest, expanding his dark T-shirt. "Don't worry. I'll protect you." He grabbed a black cowboy hat from the backseat and set it on his head, then placed a white straw hat on hers. "Wear this. I wouldn't want the hot sun to burn your cute nose."

That was thoughtful of him. "Thank you." She climbed out of the truck and headed toward the house.

"Hey, wait up. Some of those floorboards could be rotted out."

Nate hated the guy who'd bought the Double H. That idiot couldn't manage it to save his life and had let the place go to ruin. For years he couldn't do a damn thing about it, but that was about to change.

"The place isn't much to look at now," he said. "But give me six months, and I'll get it back in shape. Shane's going to help with the structural repairs."

Tori looked around. "They don't build houses like this anymore. It was meant to stand for generations." She turned to him. "I would love to see the inside."

This time Nate grinned as he slipped his hand into his jeans pocket and pulled out a key. "Whatever the lady wants."

"You're kidding. I thought the place wasn't yours yet."

He shrugged. "John Peterson at the bank has let me come out here a few times. He wants the place sold as bad as I want to buy it. Just so you know I'm not breaking and entering."

Tori had never met a more honest man. "As if you would ever break the law."

"Hey, in my younger days, I was pretty wild," he insisted as he climbed to the porch, and began checking for loose boards. Then he walked to the carved-oak-and-beveled-glass door.

"What did you do, steal an apple?" she teased.

"No, we had an orchard. But I did give Billy Lofton a black eye."

"Oh, my," she gasped, having trouble believing this man could be violent. "I'm sure you had a good reason."

He slipped the key into the lock. "I did. He made Mary Sue Newcomb cry." He looked at her, his black hat cocked low over his silver eyes. Her stomach clenched and heat slowly spread through her body. Lucky Mary Sue to have Nate champion her.

"Was she your girlfriend?"

He used his shoulder to jar the stuck door, and it finally gave way. "No, I didn't like girls in third grade. But my daddy taught me that you didn't hurt people's feelings, especially little girls' feelings. Billy needed to learn that, too."

Tori sighed. Why did she have to run into this guy? Why now?

Nate pushed open the squeaky door and motioned for Tori to go inside. She walked across the threshold and into another era. Every inch of the large room was covered in dirt, from the dull hardwood floors to the oak woodwork and staircase. Cobwebs adorned the twelve-foot ceilings, but nothing could hide the beauty underneath.

"Oh, my. This place is incredible." She walked into the living room where a huge stone fireplace nearly overwhelmed the space. She could picture a roaring fire with young Nate, Shane and Emily lying on the carpet in front of it. And on the oak mantle, a row of the Hunter family photographs.

"Be careful," he warned. "You'll get dirty."

Tori brushed her dusty hands off on the seat of her pants, then walked into the dining room. A bank of double-hung windows took up one wall, allowing in a lot of light. An antique brass chandelier hung in the center of the room, the finish dulled with years of grime.

This had been a real home, something that Tori had never had. She'd grown up in a mansion, but it had never felt like a home. Tears flooded her eyes and she hurried into the kitchen, hoping she could pull herself together. She didn't want Nate to see how pathetic she was.

Nate couldn't keep up with Tori. Her enthusiasm surprised him. He glanced around and wondered what she'd seen that he missed. The place was in surprisingly good shape structurally. The outside needed painting and the roof repaired. No doubt there was water damage upstairs, but nothing he couldn't handle. What he couldn't handle was seeing Tori's excitement. It made him think that she could possibly fit in here…with him.

You don't even own the place yet so get that notion out of your head. He walked into the kitchen and found her standing at the window. She'd taken off her hat and was wiping her eyes.

He went to her. "Tori, what's wrong?"

She immediately turned away. "Nothing," she murmured.

Nate cupped her cheek, tilted her face up and saw tears glistening in her eyes.

"Sorry, I was thinking about my childhood and the way my life has turned out."

"Hey, it's not so bad. We've all been there. Besides, you have a place to stay and soon your car will be repaired," Nate said, wishing he could spend a few minutes with the guy who'd put her in this predicament. "And you've got friends. So don't waste your time thinking about that bastard. He isn't worth your time."

In fact, Tori hadn't given Jed much thought at all. "I'm not thinking about Jed." She was embarrassed. "I was picturing your family living here." She looked up at him. "I mean, you must have so many wonderful memories."

"I do, but like most people, I didn't appreciate what I had until it was too late. When Dad died, everything changed."

She didn't say anything for a long time, then offered, "My mom died when I was seven. I don't have any brothers or sisters."

"I'm sorry, Tori," Nate said and took her in his arms. She didn't resist. It felt too good. This man had a way of making everything feel better. For the past couple of weeks her head had been occupied with thoughts of Sheriff Nate. Big, strong, tender and a great kisser. Nate Hunter.

Somehow she had to resist. She pressed her hands on his chest to put space between them, but feeling his rapid heartbeat, she paused and looked up at him. Big mistake. That didn't do anything to dampen her desire.

"I envy you so much. Not just for your family…but because you know where your life is headed. I have no idea…"

He moved back slightly, but didn't release her. "You need to give yourself time, Tori. I don't know what happened between you and this Jed guy, only that he hurt you. Just know that you have people here you can count on."

Once again emotions welled up inside her. "I've always been so busy with school and my career. I never had much chance to make many friends."

"Well, you made some here." His large hands cupped her face and his smile faded. "And you have me," he whispered and lowered his head. "Boy, do you have me."

All her resistance vanished. She parted her lips, anticipating his kiss, when a man's voice called out. Nate cursed and Tori jumped back just in time to see Shane stroll into the kitchen.

Nate's brother glanced back and forth between the two. A slow grin spread over his face as he jammed his hands in his pockets. "Hey, what are you two up to?"

Nate had always thought Shane was annoying when they were kids. But that was nothing compared to this. Shane had a bad habit of showing up at the most inopportune times.

"Thought you said you couldn't come out until four o'clock," Nate said.

Shane shrugged. "Kurt Easton showed up and started to play boss. I decided I didn't need the headache. So I let my foreman handle things." He tipped his hat back and refocused his attention. "Hello, Tori. It's nice to see you again." His gaze wandered over her. "You sure are a breath of fresh air in this old musty place."

Nate wanted to gag, then looked at Tori to find her blushing.

"Nice to see you, too, Shane," she told him. "Nate invited me out to look at the ranch. He was just telling me about his plans. This house is beautiful."

"I agree with you." Shane glanced around the old country kitchen, but his gaze returned to Tori. "Like most of us, it just needs some loving care which I plan to start working on once my brother here gives me the word."

"That's thoughtful of you," Tori said.

Shane approached Nate and draped an arm over his shoulder. "Hey, he's my big brother, what can I say?"

Nate shook off Shane's sudden show of affection, along with his arm. "We'd better get started with the measurements. I'd like some estimates on the barn before it gets too deep in here to walk."

"Just tell me where to start," Shane said.

"The barn," Nate said again, then told Tori, "You might want to stay here. I'm not sure what condition the place is in, or what we'll find inside."

"I thought you brought me out here so I could look around," she told him. "I'd like to come along."

"It's fine with me," Shane jumped in, looking down at her bare legs. "I'll go ahead and chase away the snakes and barn mice."

Nate fisted his hands. He didn't appreciate his brother's leer.

"You just keep your mind on an estimate for the barn." He took Tori's hand and headed out the back door. Silently, they walked down the path to the dilapidated structure.

Nate released her and flipped the latch to unlock the padlock. He struggled, but managed to roll back the huge door. Several birds scattered up into the loft. He turned to Tori. "Wait out here until we see if there are any creatures inside."

"Okay," she quickly agreed, suddenly not as eager to go inside.

"We'll be right back, darlin'," Shane tossed at Tori.

Irritated, Nate stalked down the center aisle as the smell of damp straw and manure assaulted his nose. The busted stalls and drooping gates broke his heart. When he reached the tack room, he glanced inside to find it in the same neglected condition.

Shane wandered up behind him. "The main beams seem to be in good shape, but I'll climb up into the loft and have a closer look. I can tell you now, the roof needs to be replaced."

Nate had trouble concentrating on the task. "What exactly were you pulling there in the kitchen?"

"What do you mean?"

"Like you don't know. Back off with Tori. She's been through a rough time, she doesn't need you hitting on her for a summer fling."

Shane acted hurt. "How do you know I'm not thinking about a permanent relationship?"

"Because I know you. Two dates with a woman and you're long gone. I don't want Tori to be one of your victims."

A slow grin lit his brother's face. "Why don't you admit that you've got the hots for her?"

"We're just friends," Nate asserted too quickly.

Shane folded his arms over his chest. "Then, if you have no claim on her, you won't care if I ask her out?" he asked as he started to walk away.

Nate grabbed his brother's arm to stop him. "Over my dead body."

Shane cocked an eyebrow. "For someone who says he isn't interested, you're pretty territorial."

Okay, so he had feelings for Tori. Nate could cope with that. "Call it what you want, just keep your distance."

Shane nodded, then pulled away. "Consider it done. Now, if there's nothing else, I'll be up in the loft checking the beams."

"No, there's nothing else."

Shane paused. "If you're smart, Nate, you'll go after Tori. Someone like her doesn't walk into your life every day."

He knew that. "She's leaving soon."

"Then give her a reason to stay." Shane smiled. "I know you're a little out of practice, bro, but you can be pretty convincing if you put your mind to it." With those words, he turned and walked to and up the loft steps.

The problem was Nate didn't have anything to offer. The Double H wasn't his yet. And the condition of the place wasn't even livable. How could he ask someone like Tori to… He stopped the direction of his thoughts and started back toward the door.

When he reached Tori, he noticed her white canvas shoes. They weren't going to stay that way for long. He looked up into her face, and found excitement in her eyes. She honestly seemed interested in the place and had never once complained about the conditions.

"It's a mess in there," he told her, but took her by the arm and walked her inside. All the time his brother's words kept ringing in his ears.

"I'm going to work on the barn first. Rebuild the stalls, then I hope to get some boarders. After that I'd like to buy a nice brood mare and some nice saddle horses. Along with a small herd of Hereford heifers, I should be able to handle the operation on my own for a while."

She looked at him. "It's a lot of work, but I have no doubt you can do it."

"Thanks for your vote of confidence," he said, suddenly realizing how much her approval had meant to him.

Once outside, at the corral, or what was left of the weathered broken fence, a flood of memories filled his head. "I wish you could have seen this place ten years ago. It sure was something."

"It still is," she said.

Nate glanced past the destruction of the barn and

corral, out to the fields of high grass sprinkled with yellow and white wildflowers. The sun reflected off the mountains in the distance. In the other direction were the two acres of apple orchard that once had produced the best Red and Golden Delicious in the area. Although the trees had been neglected, the majority were still healthy.

Suddenly he was filled with pride for his heritage. "See the apple orchard over there," he said, placing a hand on her shoulder and pointing. "With my mother's help, I think I can save most of the trees." He smiled in remembrance. "You haven't tasted anything sweeter than one of my mother's apple pies."

Tori could hear the excitement in Nate's voice. "I can only imagine how good they are."

"The best," he assured her. His hand remained on her shoulder as they continued to gaze at the pasture. "And farther toward the mountains, there's a cave and hot springs. Man, nothing like it after a long hard day. Shane and I used ride up there and strip…"

It was bad enough for Tori just standing so close to Nate. She didn't need to picture him naked. "Sounds like paradise."

"It was." He looked at her. "Next time we come out, I'll take you up there. It's about a mile hike. Think you can handle that?"

She couldn't think past the news that Nate wanted to bring her back here. "I can make it that far."

He smiled. "Good. But you'll need to wear jeans, and

I'm sure Emily has a pair of boots that would fit you. It's too bad we can't ride in on horseback. Have you ever ridden?"

She nodded, feeling the warm imprint of his hand on her back. "Yes, but it's been a few years." She hadn't been on a horse since boarding school.

"Man, my ideal woman." He winked at her. "She owns my fantasy car and knows her way around a horse."

Tori laughed, trying to keep it light. "Be careful, Sheriff, you'll turn my head."

He suddenly grew serious as he studied her. "I'm finding I want to do more than that." His gaze lowered to her mouth. "You've been distracting me since you arrived in town, Tori Sheridan." His fingers caressed her cheek. "I should be concentrating on things around here, but I'm really wondering what you think about this place."

Nate's honesty caught her off guard. Tori swallowed, torn between going with her feelings, or running before it was too late. She couldn't move. "I didn't mean to distract you, Nate. And I think this place is incredible."

"When my great-great-grandmother arrived here she said something similar. That's the reason the original homestead was called Hunter's Haven."

"The town was founded by your family?"

A slow smile appeared. "Impressed?"

She nodded, unable to speak. It took all her concentration to steady her breathing.

"The Hunters have lost so much over the years." His eyes grew fierce as he talked about his ancestors. "Land, several fortunes, lives. Ranching is a hard life and you won't ever become a millionaire at it."

"Money isn't everything," she said. "You have to do what makes you happy. And soon you'll have the Double H Ranch back."

His intense gray eyes searched her face. "Oh, Tori. You have no idea how much I want to believe that."

Nate pressed a soft kiss against her forehead, then looked down at her. The desire in his eyes was easy to read, because Tori felt the same longing. She tried to resist, but she wanted Nate just as much as he obviously wanted her. She slipped her arms around his neck, but Shane suddenly appeared in the opening to the loft.

"Hey, you two," he called out to them. "Did you forget about me?"

"You're hard to ignore, bro," Nate said as he draped an arm protectively around Tori. He liked the feeling of her pressed to him, was glad she didn't seem to want to let him go, either. Oh, yeah, he wanted Tori with him as much as possible. He might be worried about her leaving, but not right now.

"What did you find up there?" he asked his brother.

"I've got good news and bad news," Shane said. "I'll be right down."

Nate turned back to Tori. As much as he'd tried to keep things light, something was happening between them. He found he wanted to kiss that sweet mouth of hers and to caress her shapely body until she surrendered to him. Then he wanted to make love to her until they were both satisfied. Actually, he doubted he ever would be satisfied.

Tori Sheridan wasn't the type of woman you could easily walk away from.

Chapter Seven

The following afternoon, Tori had to smile at the group of teenagers who came into the café. Their laughter automatically brightened her mood, even though Nate hadn't been in at all during her shift. She shouldn't care if he hadn't stopped by to see her. Wasn't that what she wanted? An easy friendship with the man? She didn't need him to kiss her again. And he hadn't, but just twenty-four hours ago, she'd nearly kissed him. Thank goodness Shane had interrupted them, saving her from an emotional complication she couldn't afford now.

So just stop missing him, she told herself as she carried the tray full of soft drinks to the corner booth.

"Thank you, Tori," one of the girls called out.

"You're welcome."

A tall lanky boy named Jason returned from the juke-box. "Hey, Tori, when will your car be running again?"

"Ernie's found the parts. I just need money to pay him, so keep the tips coming." She winked and strolled away as Credence Clearwater's "Proud Mary" filled the café. She moved to the music as she cleared away dishes, then carried them into the back where Sam was singing along as he filled the dishwasher.

She smiled. She had the best work environment. It was almost worth the early hours and tired feet. "Here are the rest of the lunch dishes, Sam," she said.

"Thanks." He glanced at the clock. "Hey, isn't your shift over?"

"Cindy's running late. I told her I'd stay until she gets here."

Sam raised an eyebrow. "Just don't let the girl take advantage of you."

"It's not a problem. Besides, she switched days off with me so I could volunteer at the school."

Sam closed the machine. "You really like working with kids, don't you?"

She nodded and leaned against the counter to take some pressure off her tired feet. "At one time I wanted to be a teacher. I got my degree in education."

"Then why aren't you teaching?"

"I guess I wanted to try the corporate world." As usual she'd let J.C. talk her into doing what he wanted her to.

"So you gave it a shot. Now go after what you want.

Talk with Betty. I heard they're looking for a teacher to replace Miss Talbert who retired this year."

Surprisingly, Sam's suggestion excited her. "I don't know if I'll be staying…" She realized it was getting harder and harder to think about leaving this town.

"Would it hurt to ask a few questions?"

"No, it wouldn't." She went to the counter and checked to see if the customers needed anything. The kids were busy dancing. She went into the kitchen where Sam was busy going through the mail. He let out a slew of curse words as he read over a business letter, then glanced up and saw Tori.

"Sorry. I didn't plan on anyone hearing me."

"That's all right. Anything I can help you with?"

He held up the letter. "Know how to get the IRS off my back?"

"Not really. I just know they don't mess around. They can take away your home, your business. Maybe you should get a lawyer."

"That's how I got into this mess." He hesitated, then said, "I let some hotshot in Tucson handle my business affairs. He charged me a bunch of money and didn't help at all."

Tori couldn't let Sam get into any more trouble. "Would you have a problem if I took a look-see?"

When he shook his head, she opened the envelope and scanned the typed page, then sighed. Sam owed back taxes.

"Sam, it says you owe them almost thirty-five hun-

dred dollars, and they're tacking on interest as we speak."
She could get the money for him if he needed it.

He took the letter back. "I'll take care of it."

"Sam, how long have you ignored this?"

He was reluctant, but finally told her. "The waitress
you replaced, Nancy Turner, handled my books, too.
She needed the extra money I paid her to do the job.
Then, after a dozen years, she decided to go live with
her sister in Florida. She just up and told me she was
going to stop wasting her time in this dead-end job and
find a rich old man to take care of her. The marrying
kind."

Tori smiled. "Maybe she left because a certain man
didn't return her feelings."

Sam actually blushed. "It wasn't like that with
Nancy. Well, not for a long time, anyway."

"Not since you realized you have feelings for someone else. Someone like Betty Hunter, perhaps," Tori
said.

The red deepened in his cheeks. "That's a darn foolish notion. Betty and I have been friends for years. I was
friends with Ed, too."

"Ed Hunter has been gone a long time. There's no
reason Betty can't be attracted to another man."

Sam snorted. "There are about a dozen reasons. She's
college-educated, and I quit school when I was sixteen.
And she's well respected in this town."

Tori couldn't believe Sam's feelings of insecurity.
"So are you."

"She's beautiful," he continued. "And I'm a balding middle-aged man."

Tori studied Sam. His kind hazel eyes and lined face made it easy to trust him. So what if he was a little thin in the hair department? "Betty is beautiful, especially when she smiles…at you. Not every woman is only interested in the outside package, you know. It's a man's sincerity and tenderness that win a woman's heart."

Sam seemed at a loss for words. "This is foolishness." He started off toward the walk-in refrigerator, went inside and closed the door behind him. He finally came out carrying a box of lettuce. "You can leave, I'll handle things until Cindy gets here." He dropped the crate onto the counter.

She went to him. "I'm sorry that I intruded into your private life."

He nodded.

"You still should hire another bookkeeper."

His eyes lit up. "I could pay you."

Tori was touched he put such trust in her. "Sam, I could help for now…but only for a while."

He smiled. "I'll take whatever time I can get."

Tori wanted to hug this man. Not so long ago he'd helped her when she had no place to go, and she was sure she wasn't the first person he'd helped.

"Okay, I'll be your temporary bookkeeper, on one condition." When he looked at her, she went on to say, "Don't back away from your feelings for Betty." She held up her hand to stop his protest. "She cares about you, Sam, or she wouldn't treat you as part of her family. Just think about it, okay?"

He frowned. Tori knew how hard it was for him. She just prayed she was right. It wasn't as if she was an expert when it came to romance.

"Okay, but I have a condition, too," he said. "I'll give it a shot, if you'll also talk to Betty about the teaching position."

Tori felt a thrill of excitement. Could she end up teaching after all? How would Nate feel about her staying? So many thoughts flooded her head but she pushed them all aside. She had to deal with her immediate problem. "Why not?" she said. "It wouldn't hurt to ask."

By five o'clock that evening Tori had taken a shower and washed her hair to rinse away the day's grime. After dressing in a pair of jeans and a T-shirt she walked out of the tiny bathroom in search of something to eat.

She checked the shelf over her sink. It held a box of cereal and several cans of soup. None of it sounded appetizing. Usually Sam insisted she take something from the café at the end of her shift. But today they had both been too distracted by his bookkeeping fiasco to think about food.

"Well, it looks like soup tonight." She picked up a can, and was about to open it when there was a knock on the door. She smiled. Probably Sam, checking on her. It was nice to know that someone was looking out for her.

She pulled open the door, surprised to find Nate standing on the landing. He wore a pair of dark denim jeans and a starched white Western shirt. His hair was damp and he looked freshly shaven. "Nate…"

"Hi, Tori. Sorry to just show up on your doorstep, but you don't have a phone." He gave her a half smile. "Makes it a little hard to call a girl for a date."

She tried to act coolly toward him. "You could have stopped by the café."

"I've been in Tucson all day. I had to testify in a trial. Just got back about thirty minutes ago."

"Oh," was all she could manage. He'd rushed over to see her.

"Think I could come in for a minute?"

"Um—sure." She stepped aside and caught a whiff of his aftershave as he passed her. Just his presence affected her ability to think clearly, then he looked at her and she couldn't speak.

"I know it's short notice but I was wondering if you'd like to see a movie tonight."

"A movie?"

He nodded as he glanced at the counter and her unopened can of soup. "And we could get something to eat beforehand."

"Get something to eat?"

His grin was slow and easy. "Is there an echo in here?" He leaned closer and she could see tiny green specks in his eyes. "Tell me, am I doing this wrong? It's been a while since I've asked a girl out."

Nate's admission made her smile. "Oh, no. You're doing it right. I'm just surprised." And happy, she thought silently. "Yes, I would like to go to a movie." She glanced down at her attire, knowing she'd never go out in San Francisco in a pair of jeans. "Am I dressed okay?"

"You're perfect." His voice was low and husky.

She felt her cheeks redden as she went to the bed and grabbed her purse. "What's the movie?"

"Well, it's Tuesday, so it's classic movie night. *Star Wars.*"

Tori smiled. She couldn't hide her pleasure. Not just because of the movie—but she would be spending the evening with Nate.

It was just after eight o'clock when Nate bought two tickets at the theater window. He'd been so engrossed in conversation with Tori that the time had gotten away from him, almost making them late for the main feature.

Not to disturb the dozens of moviegoers, Nate took Tori's hand and led her toward the back. Once seated, he didn't release his hold on her slender hand, happy she seemed content to let him hold it.

So far this first date was going great. He'd taken Tori to the Pizza Palace for dinner. Once the other diners got over their curiosity about their budding relationship, they'd been able to enjoy their meal. But he knew that any time with Tori Sheridan would be pleasurable.

All that day in Tucson, thoughts of her had distracted

him. It had been hard to concentrate on his testimony. He couldn't stop thinking about the previous day and the time they had spent together at the Double H. How she'd listened to his hopes and dreams for the place. By the time he'd driven back to Haven this afternoon, there'd been no doubt that he'd end up on her doorstep.

And not just for tonight. He wanted to spend a lot of time with her. He didn't want to think about her leaving town. He clung to the slim hope that she might stay. He knew it was crazy. He had no business thinking about a permanent relationship with a woman. Not now. But that didn't stop this need he had to keep her here. And he liked the idea that she'd missed him today, too.

That was a start.

The theater grew silent as the picture began and the familiar words flashed across the screen… *In a galaxy far, far away…* Then the familiar battleships appeared on the screen.

Nate squeezed Tori's hand and smiled when she squeezed back. As blasts erupted on the big screen, he slid his fingers between hers, then slowly moved his hand up and down. He found he was oblivious to the action of the starship or the battle raging on the screen. All that was on his mind was Tori, her smile, her laughter when he'd described his family's antics over the years. She still hadn't had much to say about her life up to now. If he were a betting man, he'd say it had a lot to do with the sadness in her eyes. A sadness that he wanted to make disappear.

Nate raised their locked hands to his lips and placed a soft kiss against her fingers. Even with the noise of the war being fought on-screen, he heard her sharp intake of breath. Not daring a look at her, he pressed their locked hands against his thigh. Need spiraled through his body. This rush of sensation brought on a fierce hunger that was new to him, had only happened with Tori. He finally stole a glance at her and thought in the darkness that he saw the same desire mirrored in her gaze.

He wanted her as he'd never wanted another woman. He leaned toward her. "Let's get out of here."

She didn't say a word, just nodded, then let him lead her out of the theater. No words were spoken as he helped her into the truck. He hurried around to the other side. When he saw her starting to buckle her safety belt, he stopped her and pulled her to the middle of the bench seat then fastened her in next to him.

"I don't want to share you tonight." He waited for her to disagree, praying she wouldn't. "Do you have a problem with that?"

She shook her head. "No."

He started the truck. He knew he was acting crazily, but Tori Sheridan made him crazy. And he planned to enjoy every minute of the ride.

Tori was nervous as Nate drove down the alley, pulled in and parked next to the garage and his apartment.

Was she ready for this?

Nate killed the engine and they sat there in the dark for what seemed like an eternity. Then he reached over and took her hand. "I'm sorry about leaving the movie. It was just so noisy, and…I want to show you something."

Before she could protest, he'd gotten out and was helping her out of the truck. He walked her toward the steps leading to his apartment. She knew she should be panicked, but she trusted Nate. She'd been happy the past few weeks and this man had been a lot of the reason.

He surprised her when he walked off toward the garage. He opened a side door, flipped on the overhead light, and let her go inside ahead of him. The brightness caused Tori to blink, but soon she was busy taking in the surroundings.

This neat and organized area was obviously Nate's workshop. A large table took up one wall where a workbench held a saw and different types of belt sanders. A row of chisels rested in a case. Next to it were several small knives. But what caught Tori's attention were the figurines on the table.

She hurried to get a closer look at the rough carvings. "Oh, Nate. They're beautiful."

He came up beside her. "I'm not finished with these." He picked up a bird, and his expert fingers moved over each groove in the wood.

"Nate, you have an amazing talent."

He seemed embarrassed by her praise. "I don't know about that. I just enjoy working with wood."

She couldn't believe he didn't see what she did. "You really should contact an art dealer."

He shrugged. "I've always just carved for family and friends." He walked to the cupboard, opened a drawer and pulled out another carving.

"Here's one I recently finished." He handed her a honey-colored figurine. It was an angel. The delicate, angelic face had Tori immediately mesmerized. Her gaze eagerly examined the tiny praying hands, the magnificent span of the wings. The finely chiseled lines only added to the perfection of the piece. She was beginning to recognize it as Nate's signature.

"Oh, Nate. She's exquisite."

"She's yours."

Tori couldn't stop the flood of emotions as her eyes filled. Her heart pounded. "I can't accept this."

He frowned. "Why? I carved her for you."

Nate had to have spent hours on this piece. For her. No one had ever given her anything so…precious. "No one has ever given me such a special gift."

"I'm glad you like her."

She looked up and found him watching her. "You have so much talent," she whispered. "I could never do anything like this."

He went to the cabinet, then returned with a small knife. "I bet you've never tried."

"I wouldn't know where to start," she told him.

He reached for a small block of smooth wood. "Right here. Just be careful—the knife is sharp. And make your strokes going away from your body." He demonstrated by easily slicing a thin curled strip off. "Try it."

"Oh, I can't possibly do this."

"With practice you might. I was six years old when my grandfather gave me my first knife. Believe me, I was pretty lousy." He stood behind her as his arms came around her, then he put the small knife in her right hand, the block of mesquite in the other.

Then he told her, "First rule, keep your fingers out of the way."

Tori nodded, but was so distracted by his hard body pressed against hers. It took all her concentration, and his help, to make the first slice in the wood.

"The knife is so sharp." She glanced over her shoulder and saw the glaze of desire in his eyes. She quickly looked away. Her next stroke wasn't as steady, even with his large, strong hands guiding her.

"That's it," he praised as he shifted his stance. Suddenly his chest was pressed against her back. Desire coiled in her tighter than a spring, so intense that she thought she would explode any second. She stole another glance over her shoulder.

Their eyes locked, and he refused to let her go. And she didn't want him to. "You're doing great," he told her as his warm breath caressed her face.

"You're just being polite."

"No, I'm saying it because it's true, but mostly because I like having my arms around you." His head dipped toward hers, his mouth so close.

Tori kept telling herself that she didn't want his kiss, she wasn't ready, but when his lips grazed hers, she knew it was a lie. She'd been waiting for Nate Hunter's kiss all her life.

She whimpered when his lips edged closer only to tease her once again. It wasn't enough, and they both knew it. She started to turn toward him, but he held her against the table with his body pressed to her. "Nate…"

"You said you didn't want me to kiss you again." His gaze was intense. "You have to be sure this time, Tori. Because once I kiss you, I'm not going to want to stop."

Somehow she managed to whisper, "I'm sure."

The knife and wood she held dropped to the table and Nate swung Tori around. There was no hesitation as he pulled her into his arms, then his mouth was on hers. His tongue swept into her mouth, hungry to sample her sweetness. He ran his hands up and down her sides inch by inch, then cupped her bottom to bring her against his body. But it still wasn't enough.

Nate tore his mouth away and tried to smile. "I've wanted to hold you like this, kiss you for so long. Every time I saw you…whenever you were close to me."

"So did I," Tori managed as he rained kisses over her face, then finally returned to her mouth. For so long, all she could feel was hurt, but with Nate it was different and that scared her. But she didn't want to think about anything past tonight—past Nate and how he made her feel. She refused to think about anything except how much she wanted this man.

With a jolt of need, Tori answered his kisses with an

eagerness of her own, realizing suddenly how desperately she needed to be desired as much as she desired him.

Suddenly Nate pulled back then swept her into his arms. He smiled at her gasp. "I just want to get more comfortable." He carried her toward the far wall where there was a futon sofa nearly hidden in the shadowed light. Sitting down, he placed her on his lap, then took her mouth in another searing kiss.

After he broke away, he continued to frame her face with his hands. "You have no idea what you do to me."

She waited for panic to settle in, but it didn't. Even though she'd known Nate for only three weeks, from the first day, she'd trusted him.

"If I'm moving too fast, tell me," he began. "I would never do anything that you weren't ready for."

Breathless, she reached up and cupped his face. She didn't want to think about the turmoil in her life. Only now…and Nate. "You're doing everything just fine."

If this was a dream, Nate never wanted to wake up. He brought his mouth down on hers, tasting her, needing everything she was offering him. And her soft moans told him she wanted more.

He reached under her T-shirt and ran his hand up her bare skin to the delicate lacy bra that barely covered her full breasts. He eased further to find her nipple pushed taut against the silky confines. With a gasp, she arched her back, inviting him to continue his assault.

Nate wanted her. Right here, right now. His rough hands roamed over her velvet skin, her perfect breasts.

He nipped at her soft, full lips, causing her to whimper. Finally his mouth covered hers in a hungry kiss. That's when the door suddenly opened and he heard his sister call his name.

"Nate, are you in here?" Emily's voice rang through the room.

Nate cursed under his breath, then released Tori and sprang off the sofa. He tucked in his shirt and ran his fingers through his hair.

"Yeah, Emily, I'm here." He hurried out of the shadows and crossed the room to meet his obviously worried sister. "What's wrong?"

"Oh, Nate." She sighed. "I've been looking for you everywhere."

Nate gripped her hands. His sister wasn't one to come running to him without reason. "What are you doing home?"

"I needed to talk to you. I hate to ask, but I need…" Her voice faded off when she glanced toward the sofa. "Tori."

Nate watched Tori walk into the light. She had smoothed her hair as best as she could, but her lips were swollen from his kisses. "Hello, Emily."

Emily glanced at her brother, her cheeks flaming. "Nate, I'm sorry. I just barged in here… I should go. I'll talk to you later." She started to leave, but Nate pulled her back.

"Hold on, Tori and I just went to the movies tonight." He didn't feel he needed to explain his "activities" to his sister. "Just tell me why you came home from school," he said.

Emily glanced at Tori. "It can wait. I'll talk to you another time. I need to get back to Tucson."

"No, Emily. It's late and I should get home," Tori insisted. "Besides, you wouldn't be here to talk to your brother if it weren't important."

Emily opened her mouth to protest, then nodded.

"I'll get my things." Tori walked across the room, gathered up her things and headed to the door.

Nate kissed his sister on the cheek and said he'd be back in ten minutes, then followed Tori out to the truck.

After he helped her in, he climbed in the driver's side. One look across the cab told him his ache for her hadn't diminished. Wisely, he started the truck and pulled out of the driveway.

"Tori, the last thing I want is for this evening to end," he whispered.

She stole a glance at him. "Maybe it's better this way. Things were moving kind of fast."

Not for him. His fingers itched to touch her, to hold her in his arms. "Are you trying to say you didn't want me to kiss you…to touch you?"

She sighed. "No, but we have to think rationally. And what was going on back in your workshop wasn't…"

He drove down Main Street past the café, knowing that all too soon he would have to leave her. He turned the corner and parked in the alley. He reached for her and pulled her across the bench seat. "Sometimes, it's best not to think," he said as his mouth captured hers.

Tori didn't resist as she parted her lips, allowing him inside. He groaned and wrapped his arms around her, drawing her closer. Yet, it wasn't close enough. He wanted to forget everything and get lost in this woman. But he couldn't, he had other obligations. He released her.

"I guess I should take you upstairs."

Tori nodded. "Thanks for a nice evening."

By the time Nate came around to help her out of the truck she'd grabbed her purse and the figurine he had made for her off the seat. When he lifted her down her body brushed against his. He sucked in a breath and resisted pulling her back into his arms. Instead, he walked her up to her door. He kissed her softly, and made himself walk away.

With the taste of Tori's kisses still lingering on his lips, he drove back to the house, trying not to think about what might have happened tonight. He hadn't wanted a woman this badly, ever. But Emily's intrusion had forced him to remember that he had family responsibilities. For the first time in a long time, he wished he had someone to share the burden.

Someone like Tori.

Chapter Eight

Nate arrived at his mother's house in minutes. It was already after eleven and he was tired, and he hoped he wouldn't have to answer any questions about being found in a compromising situation with Tori. But his main concern was about the worry he'd seen on his sister's face.

He walked in the back door and found Emily seated at the table, drinking a cup of coffee. He nodded and went to the coffeemaker and poured himself a cup. He had a feeling that whatever she wanted to tell him, he needed to be alert.

Nate turned a chair around and straddled it, then braced himself. "Okay, Em, what's so important that you needed to see me tonight?"

"Nate, I'm so sorry. I would have never barged into your workshop if…"

He raised a hand to stop her. "It's okay. Now spill it, Em. What's going on?"

She sighed. "First, if I had any other options, I wouldn't come to you."

"Em, you're scaring the hell out of me. Just tell me."

"I need a car. Mine finally broke down. The mechanic said that it wasn't worth fixing any more." Tears pooled in her eyes. "I know I've asked so much from you and money is tight, but I can't work my waitress job without a car."

He was so relieved he wanted to hug her. "That's it?"

"That's a lot. I'd give up my summer class at UCLA, but I can't get your money back."

"Will you stop, Em? You're not going to give up school—not when you're so close to graduating." He was going to take care of her. "Don't worry, I'll handle the rest," he told her. "I'll find you another car, just give me a few days."

So things were going to be tight for a while. What else was new? This was going to cut into the money he had saved for the auction, but it couldn't be helped.

"Thanks, Nate. I promise I'll pay you back."

He reached out and tugged on her long hair. "I won't hold my breath."

"Hey, one day I'm going to be rich and famous. Wait until I sell my screenplay. Then you'll be eating those words."

He knew his sister had been working on the story of four generations of the Hunter family since she'd been in high school. He prayed that her dream would come true. "Like I said, I won't hold my breath," he teased her.

His thoughts turned to his own dreams. A picture of Tori came to mind. A pizza and a movie was suddenly a luxury. And Tori Sheridan was a luxury he couldn't afford.

The next afternoon, Tori was seated at Sam's desk in the back room. She'd been working on the café's books. Her shift had ended an hour ago, but she didn't mind putting in the extra time.

Tori had also completed some personal business that had been long overdue. She'd been living in Haven close to a month and had decided it was time she settled in a little more. She knew she wasn't returning to San Francisco in the foreseeable future. No longer was she going to be J. C. Sheridan's pawn, but she'd worked hard for her salary at Sherco and she wanted access to her money. Having it would mean she could start a new life for herself. Wherever that might be.

First thing after her shift ended, she'd called her bank to transfer the substantial balance in her individual account to a Tucson bank that had a local branch in Haven, and requested a replacement for her personal credit card. Even if it would alert her father to her whereabouts, she needed to be independent.

She'd managed to live on what she made at the café,

but she hated not being able to pay her debts. Ernie had been great about buying the Corvette's parts, but he needed to be paid and soon. In about a week she'd have her money.

She had several options, one of which was staying here in Haven. She hadn't had a problem working at the café, but she needed to think about the future. A place of her own, and as Sam had suggested, possibly getting a teaching job. A good start might be working on her teaching credentials.

Another option was to go to Tucson and stay in the software business. She quickly rejected that idea. She'd made friends here. Immediately, Nate came to mind as he had several times during the long, lonely night, and later during her busy morning shift.

Heat rose to her face as she remembered the feelings he created in her. They couldn't seem to get near each other without setting off sparks. His warmth, his words of tenderness, his kisses, set off a thudding rhythm in her pulse. She shivered, knowing that making love to this man would be incredible. The idea also terrified her. What if she made another mistake?

Her thoughts turned to the beautiful angel figurine she'd placed next to her bed, the one Nate had carved for her. Her heart soared.

He was so talented. He should be showing his work. Besides, the money he could make would go a long way toward making his costly dream of restoring the Double H come true. She picked up the phone, dialed information and got the number for her friend's gallery in Monterey.

"Seaside Gallery, Audrey Brighton speaking."

"Audrey, it's Tori Sheridan."

"Oh, my goodness, Tori. It's been so long. You better be calling to say you're in town. We need to catch up. I'm dying to know why you were a no-show at your wedding."

Tori tensed. Leave it to Audrey to speak her mind. "Let's just say I came to my senses and leave it at that."

"Well, it's about time. Just tell me, are you happy?"

Tori didn't even need to think about that one. "I'm getting there, and considering a career change."

"You can come stay with me."

What a good friend. "Thanks, Audrey, but I need to do this on my own. I'd appreciate if you didn't let my father know you've talked with me."

"Consider my lips sealed. Now tell me the reason you called."

"I found a wonderful artist. His carvings are incredible."

The conversation went on for another fifteen minutes as Tori described Nate's work. Before Tori hung up the phone, Audrey agreed to take a look at some figurines, then she would make a decision.

Tori was excited about the prospect of sending Nate's work to Audrey. He deserved to have his talent discovered. Tori had never met a nicer man, or a sexier one. She thought back to his kisses, to the way he held her, had touched her last night, and a shiver ran through her.

But was it too soon to have feelings for Nate? A person didn't fall in love in a matter of weeks. Did they? She definitely had to slow things down. She wasn't ready to start up a relationship with another man. Was she?

Lost in her thoughts, she barely heard Sam call to her. "Sorry. What did you say, Sam?"

He leaned against the desk. "Would you run an errand for me?"

"Sure." She picked up the stack of checks she'd written out and had Sam sign. "I need to go to the post office first. Where to?"

"The Hunters. Emily is home for the day, so I cooked her favorite meal. You can take my truck."

A rush of excitement surged through Tori. "You don't want to take it yourself?"

"Can't. I'm expecting a shipment. I guess you'll have to do the honors. If you don't mind?"

"Sure, I don't mind." Maybe she'd see Nate. All day she'd longed for him to walk into the café, but she knew he had a lot on his mind right now. This would be a good time to show Nate that they needed to be just friends for now. The problem was how could she convince him when she wasn't sure a platonic relationship was what she really wanted.

Nate hadn't stopped thinking about Tori since he'd left her at her apartment the night before. By the time he'd finished talking with Emily and got a few hours sleep, he had to go back on duty. He would have called Tori if she had a phone but she didn't. In any case, a telephone chat wouldn't have stopped his mind from wandering back to last night, or the pure pleasure of having her in his arms. Things had been perfect. She'd been perfect. He'd get lost in his daydreams featuring Tori and then reality would hit. He simply had too many commitments already to even consider asking Tori to be part of his life.

Nate turned the patrol car into his driveway. He'd stop at his mother's house just long enough to grab something to eat and say hello to Emily. When he saw Sam's truck he smiled. More than likely the older man's visit included something good to eat.

He opened the back door and walked into the kitchen. "Hey, I hope you guys left enough for me. I didn't get a chance for lunch, and I'm starved—"

He stopped when he saw Tori in the crowd around the table. Everyone else in the room disappeared and his heart rate shot up. She looked fresh and pretty in her yellow print blouse and white slacks. Her hair lay in soft waves against her shoulders. Her eyes, a rich honey-brown, had him craving her instantly. Every rational thought disappeared from his head. He wanted this woman more than he wanted his next breath and that thought nearly staggered him.

"Hi, Tori. I… I didn't expect to see you here."

Tori couldn't control the blush that spread over her

face. This wasn't how she wanted to see Nate again, not surrounded by his family. And by the look on his face, she judged he wasn't crazy about seeing her again so soon, either. "I just dropped off dinner from Sam." She stood up. "Well, I should get back."

It was Shane who reached for her hand. "No, darlin', you aren't going anywhere. You're staying for dinner," he said and glared at Nate. "Unlike some people."

"Oh, no, there's plenty for everyone," Tori said. "You included, Nate." Feeling awkward, she couldn't look him in the eye. What did she expect, that he would sweep her into his arms? "I have more errands to run. I hope you enjoy it, Emily."

"I'll stop by and see you at the café before I leave in the morning," the younger girl called.

Tori smiled. "Sure. Bye, everyone."

Nate reached for her. "Don't leave."

She finally looked at him. "I have to." She hurried out the door hoping he wouldn't come after her. These glimpses of the perfect family were too much of a reminder of what she didn't have…what she longed to have.

"Tori, wait," Nate called to her, but she kept on going until she reached the truck. She started the engine, but found she couldn't leave. Nate's patrol car blocked her exit.

Nate reached the truck and stepped up on the running board. "Please, Tori. Don't go." His gaze met hers. "We need to talk."

"What about? How awkward you feel about me

showing up at your house?" she said, recalling his shocked look. "It's a little embarrassing when your sister catches us…together, but it's ten times worse when the next day you act as if you barely know me."

"I was caught off guard."

"Well, it won't happen again. Move your car and let me leave." She released a long breath. "Just do me a favor and stop showing up at my door. I don't know how to play these games." She gripped the steering wheel. "Maybe last night I let you do…"

"Don't, Tori." He yanked open the truck door, and slid in beside her. "Dammit, I wanted you last night, I wanted you this morning and I still want you now."

Her eyes widened. "Then…why?"

He shrugged. "I saw you talking with my family. You just fit in so perfectly. But my life isn't perfect."

Nate chanced looking at her. That pretty face, those tawny eyes that haunted him. "You've seen the condition of the ranch I'm trying to buy back. And I have commitments to my family. I can't make any promises just now."

"I don't remember asking you to make any. My life isn't exactly settled, either. I need to make plans for my future, too. And I don't know if I'll be staying in town."

His arm came around her, his mouth inches from hers. "Tori, I know I don't have the right to ask, but I don't want you to leave." He covered her mouth with his, stopping any protest, hoping to take away her anger, praying he could persuade her. Suddenly he heard the squawking of his patrol car radio. He broke off the kiss, but didn't let go of her.

"Nate, you need to answer that."

"Not until you agree to spend tomorrow afternoon with me at the ranch."

Tori knew she'd be better off walking away, but God help her, she didn't want to. She wanted to be with Nate. She wanted hear about his hopes and dreams for the ranch, mostly she wanted to be part of his life, if only for a little while.

When she nodded, he rewarded her with his grin, then he kissed her hard and fast. Just as suddenly, he broke it off and got out. She sat there motionless, listening to his patrol car start up and back out of the drive then race off down the street.

She blew out a long breath and was about to start the truck when she remembered the reason she'd wanted to come by the Hunters'. She went back to the house and Betty appeared at the screen door.

"Tori, good, you didn't leave," she said and opened the door to let Tori inside the now-empty kitchen.

"If you have a minute I'd like to talk to you about Nate's carvings. I called a friend of mine who's an art dealer. She wants to see a sample of his work. Normally, she'd take slides or pictures, but she's having a new-artist show this weekend. Since there's no time, she's willing to take a look at his carvings right away."

Tori hoped she hadn't overstepped any family boundaries. "I was wondering how to approach Nate about it."

"Don't. Not yet," Betty said. "If your friend likes what she sees, then we'll tell Nate."

Tori wasn't sure she agreed. "Then how am I going to get some samples of his work?"

Betty led her into the living room and to the glass cabinet. "Take your pick."

Tori raised an eyebrow. "Oh, Betty, are you sure?"

"Yes, I want the world to see my son's talent." She opened the door and took out the proud eagle and predatory wolf. "It's about time he worked on his dream. And you can make a big part of it come true."

Looking into the other woman's face, Tori realized that Betty Hunter wasn't just talking about the Double H Ranch.

The next afternoon Tori, dressed in jeans, a long-sleeved blouse and a pair of buckskin boots she'd borrowed from Emily, could barely contain her excitement about spending the day with Nate. She was waiting for him on the porch and was surprised when he pulled into the parking space towing a long horse trailer.

He got out and climbed the steps to her, looking just as sexy as a cowboy ever could. Then he grinned and she nearly melted on the spot.

"Hi," he said, then pulled her into his arms and covered her mouth with his. She only had time to slip her arms around his neck and hang on for the sensual ride. By the time he released her she was swaying.

"Hello to you, too," she murmured.

"You ready to go?" he asked.

"Just about." She grabbed a canvas tote and her purse

and locked the door. "I have some sandwiches and drinks for the trip."

"Good, the ride will give us an appetite." Smiling, he walked her down the steps. "I have someone I want you to meet." He led her to the horse trailer where a large dapple-gray head poked out the side opening. Nate rubbed the horse's nose. "Pepper, meet Tori."

The horse bobbed its head. "Oh, how beautiful." Tori raised an eyebrow. "A mare or stallion?"

"Gelding," Nate said. "I borrowed him from a friend for the day. We'll have to ride double, which can be a lot of fun, so that way I can show you more of the ranch."

The drive to the Double H took about thirty minutes. Nate had Pepper out of the trailer, saddled and ready to go in another ten.

"It's been years since I've ridden," Tori said excitedly. "I can't believe you did this."

"I like doing things for you," he said, his gaze intense. "And I sure as hell wish I could do more than just take you for a ride…."

She was starting to care a lot about this man. "I don't want or need anything more than this beautiful afternoon. Thank you for sharing it with me. No one has ever given me such a nice gift."

"I'm just glad you're here with me." Nate started to move closer, then stopped. "We'd better mount up. Time is a wastin'," he said and wondered, not for the first time, what kind of man her ex had been to make Tori feel she wasn't worth the best.

He pushed Tori's straw cowboy hat farther down on her head, cupped his hands together and helped her up on Pepper, then swung up behind her. Taking the reins, he turned Pepper toward the open pasture and onto the narrow trail. With Pepper bearing the weight of two of them, it was going to be a slow, easy walk, but this was the best way he could give Tori a good look around.

"Where are we headed?"

"You'll see. Just sit back and enjoy the scenery." He felt her relax against his chest. He took a deep breath and inhaled her fresh scent. The softness of her hair tickled his chin. Who was he kidding? Tori Sheridan was impossible to ignore, and this was going to be a very long ride.

Finally they reached the old cabin, or what was left of the wood-and-stone structure.

"This is the original homestead, where my great-great-grandparents lived when they first came to the valley." He walked the horse to the old wrought-iron hitching post and climbed down, then helped Tori off.

The place wasn't large. Just a two-room cabin, with a sagging porch and most of the roof gone. "Someday I plan to restore this place, too." He nodded to the left. "Over there is the family cemetery. Most of my ancestors are buried there."

"Do you have a lot of family in the area?"

"Not many of us left. My dad had a brother, but years ago he sold his part of the ranch and moved to Florida."

"Did you ever want to leave?"

Nate nodded. "In college, I wanted to be anywhere but here. I hated ranch work. I wanted to see what else was out there. I'll always regret that time. My father needed me to help run this place, but I had other plans. He lost the ranch because of me."

"Oh, Nate. Don't say that. Your father loved you and wanted you to have a good life. You were just out of college and you had a right to choose your path."

"Yes, but he mortgaged the ranch to pay for my college." Nate grabbed the horse's reins, led him to the water trough and began to pump the well.

Tori followed. "I think we all feel we owe our parents for the sacrifices they make for us." A stream of clear water spurted into the bucket. "But they want us to be successful—independent."

Lord, she was none of those things. But Nate was. "Your father would be proud of you, especially of how you've stepped in to help your family."

A faint smile appeared on his face. "You think so?"

She nodded. "You don't need me to tell you that."

His silver gaze studied her. "But yours is the only opinion that matters."

She couldn't draw her breath. It was trapped somewhere in her lungs.

He moved closer. "You matter to me, Tori." He bent his head and closed his mouth over hers in a tender kiss. An achingly tender kiss. Finally he inched back. "A lot."

"Oh, Nate…" She was taking the next step, taking a

big risk by letting this man into her life. But she couldn't walk away. "You matter to me, too."

"I was hoping you would say that." He took her hand. "Come on, I want to show you a special place."

After mounting Pepper, they rode toward the foothills. Five minutes later they were in a wooded area with a trickling stream that ended up in a pool. Nate reined in the horse by a group of trees and they climbed down. Then he removed the saddle and spread the horse blanket beside the rocky edge of the pool.

Tori sat by the bank and dipped her hand in. "Oh, it's hot."

"That's because it's a hot spring. Want to go in?"

"I don't have a suit."

He smiled. "Who said you need a suit?"

She tried not to think about being naked with him. "I do."

He grinned as he opened the saddlebag and pulled out a black nylon one-piece swimsuit. "It's Emily's."

"Lord, your family must think I'm an orphan." She did have a bathing suit back in her apartment, but this suit covered a whole bunch more than her bikini did.

"They think a lot of you, and have informed me I'd better not mess up with you." His expression grew serious. "I'm going to try my darnedest not to." He gave her the suit. "You can go behind that tree to change," he teased.

As much as Tori wanted to, she was still leery about trusting again. But there was no doubt she was already half in love with this town, the Hunter family and Nate.

"You know, sitting in this spring can be considered medicinal," Nate said. "People pay big bucks to soak in a natural hot spring. What do you say?"

Unable to resist his offer, Tori went behind the large tree he indicated and changed into the borrowed suit. It was a good fit, but her pale skin somewhat ruined her sexy bathing-beauty image.

Too late to change her mind, Tori thought, and she came out from her hiding place to find Nate standing beside the pool in a pair of dark boxer trunks.

He whistled softly. "That suit never looked that good on my sister."

"Thank you." She laughed nervously, trying to ignore his wide muscular shoulders and chest. "My body is a little sun-deprived."

He walked toward her. "I'm feeling a little deprived myself." He drew her against him and kissed her, then he scooped her up into his arms.

She gasped as her arms went around his neck. "Nate, put me down," she demanded weakly.

"I plan to…" He maneuvered over the rocks, carefully stepped down into the spring and lowered them both into the shallow, warm water.

"Oh, my, it's a little startling at first."

He didn't release her as he rested along the shallow edge. She sat on his lap and the warm water rose to her breasts. "Give yourself a minute, then you'll feel you've gone to heaven."

Being in Nate's arms made her feel that way already.

Just as he could make her tense and achy, he could also make her feel lighthearted and yet safe. She closed her eyes and laid her head against his broad shoulder.

It was Nate who finally broke the silence. "Being here with you is what I call perfect." His hands moved over her back and her arms, causing a rush of sensation.

She couldn't help tilting her head up to find his mouth right there to meet hers. He urged her lips apart and deepened the kiss. She was a ready participant as she pressed her body against his.

At Tori's willing surrender, Nate's need grew. He trailed kisses across her cheek and down her neck, her murmers of pleasure driving him on.

"Tori…" He whispered her name and those incredible golden brown eyes opened to him. "I want to touch you…everywhere." When she didn't resist, he eased the thin black strap down her arm inch by agonizing inch until he exposed her breasts.

"You're so beautiful." His voice was shaky as he feasted on her perfection, then leaned down and placed a kiss against the crest of her breast and felt her tremble. He drew an unsteady breath, then traced his finger over her delicate skin.

"Please," she cried and arched closer.

He didn't hesitate and captured one of the puckered buds in his mouth. Tori whimpered again as her hands played in his hair.

Nate returned to her mouth. The kiss wasn't gentle. Their desire had been building so long that their need was too urgent to control. Her lips were soft and searing at the same time, driving him out of his mind.

"I want you, Tori." He worked to lower her suit more, but the water resisted his efforts as the material clung to her skin. That was when he heard Tori's plea.

"No, Nate. We can't," she whispered.

He raised his head and saw both the desire and panic in her eyes. Her own fingers shook as she covered his. "It's too fast." She squeezed her eyes shut. "I'm sorry. I'm just not ready for this."

Nate was having trouble checking his urges, but he forced himself to stop. He didn't want to push Tori into something she wasn't ready for. "It's okay, sweetheart." He blew out a long breath and pulled her to him, her pounding heart thudding against his.

"So, this guy you almost married. You still have feelings for him?"

She raised her head, those incredible eyes locked with his. "No. Jed never made me feel this way. I've never felt this way about anyone."

"I haven't, either."

She tried to smile. "It's only been a month, Nate. And I nearly made a big mistake. If we can just go a little slower…"

Nate's body didn't feel the same hesitancy, not with Tori on his lap. He cupped her face and kissed her softly. "We can go as slow as you want." Saying the words was difficult. "But maybe we shouldn't tempt fate." He lifted her up and out of the water. "And it will help me tremendously if you would go and get dressed."

She nodded and stood up, giving him a view of her perfect body. With his pulse racing, Nate wondered what it would take to keep Tori in town...and in his life forever.

Twenty minutes later, Tori was sitting on the small horse blanket, sharing a sandwich and the sunny afternoon with Nate. But she had some questions for the man she'd come to care about so deeply.

"Nate, why isn't there someone special in your life?"

He shrugged. "There's been a few."

Typical man, he revealed as little as possible about his romantic past. "I mean, has there been anyone special that you wanted to spend your life with?"

"There was someone in college. We'd planned to marry, but things changed. I was injured and lost my chance to play pro football." His eyes met hers. "Let's just say that Allison wasn't cut out for ranch life."

There was a long silence. Tori couldn't believe that any woman would pass up Nate's love. "Do you still have feelings for her?"

"No." A slow grin appeared and he laughed. "You sure are curious about my past."

Tori shrugged and pretended to concentrate on her sandwich. "Just making conversation."

There was a long pause before Nate spoke. "Okay, enough about our pasts," he said. "It's time for now and the future. Have you decided about staying?" He raised a hand. "And don't say you don't know yet. You strike me as the type of person who needs a plan."

"Why do you think that?"

"I've seen how you've organized your tiny apartment. At the café, you've helped Sam clean up his bookkeeping."

Nate Hunter had learned things about her that no one else ever bothered about. "You're very observant."

He winked. "I'm a cop. It's my job." His gaze softened, along with his voice. "You have to know I want you to stay here in town. But I'm also realistic, and know you had a life in San Francisco. Haven isn't San Francisco."

Her heart pounded erratically. "That doesn't mean that Haven doesn't have a lot to offer."

He put his soda can down and reached for her. Tori didn't have time to resist him before his mouth covered hers in an all-consuming kiss. One that left her breathless and not thinking about leaving any time soon. "Dammit, Tori, tell me what I can do to keep you here."

Love me, Tori's heart whispered. "Put in a good word for me to get the teaching position at the school?"

A big grin appeared across his face. "I guess I could do that. I do have a few connections." His gaze lowered to her mouth. "It's going to cost you, though."

When Nate's mouth captured hers again, Tori realized she would pay anything.

Chapter Nine

A week later, Tori smiled as Nate walked into the café. Since their trip out to the ranch they'd spent a lot of time together. There had been dinners at the Hunters' home and playing cards with the family. They'd even made it back to the theater and watched *Star Wars* all the way through.

As much as Tori wanted Nate she was still learning to trust herself and her feelings—she knew she needed to make some decisions about her future. So she'd talked with Betty about the teaching position at Haven Elementary. Actually, Betty had helped Tori arrange an interview with the school's principal about the opening for the fifth-grade teacher.

She was putting down roots. She felt as if she fitted

in here. And oh, yes, she was falling in love with Nate. Although he hadn't revealed his feelings to her, she knew he cared about her, too. Just, right now, his focus was on the upcoming auction Saturday. Once he got the ranch, she hoped things would go further between them. She wanted to be the woman who helped him rebuild the Double H. Somehow living on that ranch and having a home and family had become her dream, too.

After clearing a table, she walked back to the counter and refilled Nate's tea. In his uniform, he looked very official and very sexy.

"How can you keep the streets safe if you're sitting in here?" she teased.

"I have very efficient deputies. Besides, criminals can lurk anywhere. Even here. Maybe I should check in the back there just to make sure." Nate stood, took hold of her hand and pulled her through the kitchen into the back. Once alone, he drew her into his arms, and captured her mouth in a hungry kiss, one that curled her toes, then worked its way upward, weakening her knees. By the time he released her she had trouble seeing clearly.

Nate sighed, pressing his forehead against hers. "I've been wanting to do that since I walked in here. I just couldn't wait any longer."

Her stomach did a somersault. "I've missed you, too."

He nipped at her mouth. "Maybe we should do something about that." He pressed his aroused body against hers. "Maybe I'll take you back to the workshop and give you another lesson on whittling."

"Oh, yes." She drew a breath. "You're such a good teacher."

"Oh, darlin', that was just the first lesson." He started to kiss her again when his radio crackled. "Duty calls. See you in about an hour." He kissed her quickly and walked out the back door to his patrol car.

"Are you going to stand there all day?"

Tori turned to see Sam smiling. "Sorry, I'll get back to work."

"Not a problem, the café's empty. Why don't you take off a little early? I can handle things here so you can go get ready for your date."

"How do you know I have a date?"

He laughed. "It was an easy guess since Nate has been glued to the counter every day for the last few weeks. And if that kiss was any hotter this place would go up in flames."

She gasped as her face heated up. "Oh, Sam. You must think I'm acting crazy."

"No, I think you're acting like a woman in love."

Suddenly she felt a little breathless. "It's too soon."

He frowned. "It's not when you meet the right person. The first day you arrived I could see that Nate felt something for you. I'm just glad things worked out between you. You both deserve it. Now, get out of here and go get ready for your man."

Tori liked the sound of that. "Thank you."

She gathered her things and headed out the back door then up the stairs to her apartment. Once inside, she removed her soiled apron, then went to the small closet and examined her meager wardrobe. Finally she pulled out a fresh pair of khaki slacks and a lime-green cotton polo shirt. She'd started into the bathroom when she heard a knock on the door.

She smiled. Nate. She didn't mind that he was early. She swung open the door, but instead of her date, she found an older distinguished-looking man with dark brown hair streaked with gray.

In lieu of his usual custom-made suit and silk tie, he had on dark trousers and a wine-colored silk shirt. But J. C. Sheridan never looked anything but impressive.

"Hello, Father," she managed after a moment of stunned silence.

"Victoria." He didn't look any happier to see her than she was to see him. "Do you have any idea how much trouble you've caused me?"

As usual J.C.'s cruel words landed with a blow. But this time she wasn't going to let it bother her. She wasn't the same person who'd left San Francisco a month ago.

"What do you want?"

"Where are your manners? I came all this way and you don't even invite me inside?"

Reluctantly, she stepped aside to allow him in. He wasn't even subtle as he looked around her living quarters with obvious disgust.

"My God," he groaned. "This is a hell hole."

She took a long breath. "If you don't mind, this is my

home. It might not be up to your standards, but it suits me just fine."

"You can't tell me you're happy here. Not when you could be living in your two-thousand-square-foot condo in the best city in the country. By comparison this is a closet in Hicksville."

Why try to explain her reasons? He would never understand. "You gave me no choice."

"Okay, you've made your point, Victoria. It's time to come home. Jed is willing to forgive you—"

"Forgive me!" Tori cried. "Jed has nothing to forgive me for. I sent back his ring and told him I wasn't going to marry him because I refuse to be a pawn in a business merger." She was on the verge of tears, but she fought them with everything she had. It made her sad that her own father cared more about his company than her happiness. "No. I'm not going back." She folded her arms. "Just how did you find me, anyway?"

"Jamison Parks at the bank knew how distraught I've been since you disappeared—"

"So he broke the law and fed you personal information. Well, you can see that I'm fine and now you can return to San Francisco."

"Not without you. Sherco needs you."

It hurt that her father never once said that *he* needed her. "You have a dozen people who can replace me."

"But they aren't family. You, I trust."

She didn't trust him. "I'm sorry. I have other plans."

"Being a waitress in a greasy spoon? How could you

humiliate me like this? Have you forgotten what the Sheridan name stands for?"

How could she? J.C. had never let her forget. The Sheridan name had been all she'd thought about her entire life, but no more. "For the first time in my life, I know who I am. And I won't be a waitress forever. I'm finally going to do what I've always wanted to do, teach."

He looked relieved. "Then come back to San Francisco. I'll get you a teaching job."

"So you can manipulate me again? No, Father, my life is here." She walked to the door and opened it. "You have to leave now. I've made plans with a friend."

J.C. stood his ground. "We're not finished."

She gripped the doorknob tighter. "I'm not changing my mind."

She watched his jaw tense, then he finally walked to the door. "And I'm not leaving you here, Victoria."

"It's not your decision."

"We'll see about that," he said and marched out.

Tori closed the door and sank against it. She had actually stood up to J.C., but her high spirits quickly faded. She wasn't foolish enough to think her father didn't mean business. And that was what frightened her.

When Saturday morning finally arrived, Nate drove out to the ranch. The auction wouldn't begin until nine o'clock, but he wanted to get there early, mostly to see who else was interested in the property. He knew he had a set amount he could spend today, so if the bids went over his limit he'd be sunk.

"Would it be a waste of my breath to tell you to stop worrying?" Tori asked.

"Probably."

Nate glanced across the seat of his truck at Tori. She was a pretty sight to look at first thing in the morning. Hell, she was pretty to look at any time. He could get lost in those brown eyes of hers. And he itched to run his fingers through her soft yellow hair. When she smiled at him he felt he could conquer anything.

She took his hand. "It's going to be okay, Nate."

He pulled off the highway. "What if it isn't?"

She shook her head. "You can't think that way, Nate. Half the town is behind you on this. They want to see you get the Double H nearly as much as you do. And you haven't heard that anyone else is interested in the property, have you?"

He drove under the gate's sagging archway. "No." He knew that Kurt Easton would love to get his hands on this place, but since all his money was tied up in the new housing development, he wouldn't be a problem.

"Will you look at that," Tori said, pointing to the large group of people in the front yard.

Nate parked and turned off the engine. He recognized most of them—other ranchers, friends of his dad and many townspeople, including Sam.

"They care about you, Nate."

Emotions clogged his throat as Nate climbed out of

the truck. After greeting people and accepting pats on the back, he took Tori's hand and walked up to the table to sign up for the auction. He wanted her close. If everything went well today, he might ask her to stand by his side permanently.

The next hour passed slowly, and Tori tried to keep Nate distracted until the auctioneer found his way to a podium on the porch. The crowd quieted, and the bidding began on several pieces of farm equipment left behind from the previous owner.

"Okay, now we'll get down to business," the auctioneer began. "We have ten sections of prime land that includes a natural spring, two acres of apple orchards, a four-thousand-square-foot house and large barn." Then the auctioneer gave a base asking price from the bank and Nate raised his hand.

For what seemed like an eternity no one said a word. It began to look as if Nate was going to get his dream. Then the auctioneer pointed to a hand-raised bid from someone in the back of the crowd. Tori felt Nate tense, then raised his arm to counter the bid. The other bidder raised again.

Tori glanced over her shoulder and searched the crowd for the person who was hindering Nate's dream. She froze when she saw a familiar face. The middle-aged man was dressed in casual slacks and an open-collared sport shirt. She gasped when she realized that she knew him. It was Trent Knox. He worked for her father at Sherco. But she already knew what he was doing here. Her father had brought him in. She had to put a stop to this.

Nate was engrossed in the action, so she stepped back, and slipped through the crowd. That was when she saw her father standing against the fence.

She marched toward him. "What are you doing?"

His face was impassive. "Just looking around for some investments."

"Well, you can look somewhere else."

He glanced around. "I like this place."

Tori gasped as the auctioneer recognized Knox's next bid.

Her father glanced down at her. "You want me to stop? There is a way, you know. Come back to work."

"I told you I don't want to."

The auctioneer had Nate's bid. "Going once, twice…"

Knox raised his paddle and the auctioneer took his higher bid.

"Please, stop this," she begged her father. "You don't care about this place, but Nate wants his family ranch back."

"And I want my daughter back," he demanded.

Tori knew that Knox would follow J.C.'s instructions and go the limit on this. And Nate would lose his dream. She couldn't let that happen.

Nate countered the bid and Knox was about to raise his paddle when Tori grabbed her father's arm. "I'll go back, but only until the merger is completed."

J.C. hesitated, then signaled to Knox that he was

done. The auctioneer's gavel hit the podium awarding the ranch to Nate.

But at what cost to Nate, and what cost to her?

Nate accepted the congratulations as he walked up to the cashier. He wasn't sure if he was happy or not. The price was several thousand more than he wanted to pay. In fact, he wasn't sure if the bank would cover his loan.

He couldn't hide his curiosity about the stranger bidding against him. But after looking around, he couldn't find him—or Tori. After he finished the paperwork, he turned around to see her standing beside an older man. He had no idea who the man was, but he was determined to find out. "Tori," Nate called as he walked up to her.

She smiled nervously. "Congratulations, Nate. You got the Double H back."

"It was a little pricey, but worth it." He looked at the stranger. "Hello, I'm Nate Hunter." He held out his hand.

"J. C. Sheridan. I'm Victoria's father."

Nate tensed. So her father had come after her. Nate held out his hand. "Pleased to meet you, sir. Guess you didn't expect to find your daughter at an auction."

Sheridan shrugged. "I heard about the auction in town, and decided to come out and have a look. But mostly, I wanted to see my daughter and bring her home."

Nate stiffened. "Wouldn't that be Tori's decision?"

Sheridan smiled slowly. "Oh, I think she's come to her senses."

Tori turned to her father. "Please, Father, I'd like to talk with Nate alone."

Sheridan looked Nate up and down, then finally he nodded before he walked to a large black town car.

Nate turned to Tori. "He's blowing smoke, right?"

She didn't look him in the eyes. "He needs me, Nate. I've been his assistant for the last two years. I know this merger inside out. I've worked day and night on it for months."

"Then let someone else learn it. I thought you wanted a life here." He'd gotten his hopes up that she wanted him, too.

"Would you walk away from your job if I asked you?"

"It would depend on the reason. Besides, you walked away before we ever met."

"And I need to go back…temporarily. It's only six months. I can come back."

Nate was hurt. What a fool he'd been. He had this crazy notion that she might be happy here. "Was this what you wanted all along, Tori, for Daddy to come chasing after you?"

He saw her shock, but she quickly masked it. "My mistake. I never knew you thought so little of me." She took a long breath. "I guess the only thing to say is goodbye."

His chest hurt and he fought to keep from reaching for her and begging her to stay. "I guess so."

"Nate. Thank you for everything you've done."

He didn't want her damn gratitude. "If I hadn't been

around, you'd just have had to call Daddy sooner?" He gave a sarcastic laugh, fighting his anger. "This must've all been a game to you. String the small-town sheriff along."

Tears pooled in her eyes as she tried to reach for him. He jerked away. "Please, Nate. It wasn't like that. I truly care about you."

He couldn't do this anymore. "Well, have a nice life, Tori. And if you're ever stuck on the highway again… call Daddy and save us all a lot of trouble."

Chapter Ten

By that afternoon Tori had packed up her things. She only had the one suitcase, but she wanted to take everything. She glanced at the small table beside the bed where she used to keep her carved angel. Once back in San Francisco, she'd contact Audrey to make sure that the figurine was returned to her there. It was the one special memory she would keep of Nate.

Fighting tears, she gave the bag to her father's driver and glanced around the small, dingy room. In the last month, it had become her home. Finally she closed the door and trudged down the stairs to the café's back door.

That was where she found Sam, in the kitchen getting ready for the supper crowd. He glanced in her direction. For the longest time neither one of them spoke.

"So you're really leaving," he finally said.

She nodded and held out the apartment key. "I just wanted to return this." When he didn't take it, she set it down on the counter. "Sam, I can't thank you enough for all you've done for me."

He shook his head. "Don't give me so much credit. Nate talked me into giving you a job, and into letting you stay upstairs. He also got Ernie to trust you for the car repairs. I just got lucky and got a good waitress out of the deal and…a good friend." He studied her. "I'm going to miss you."

"Please, Sam. Don't make this any harder than it already is. This is the way it has to be."

"You're the one who's making it hard, Tori. If you wanted to go back to San Francisco so bad, you could have left a long time ago."

She couldn't tell Sam the truth. "It's what I want now."

"Tori, how can you let that man steal your happiness?"

She couldn't talk about it. "Heather Johnson has offered to work my shifts for the rest of the summer until she goes back to school. I've got to go, Sam."

Before she could turn away, he grabbed her in his burly arms and hugged her close. "You are so special, Tori Sheridan. I just hope one day you realize that."

She held on to Sam like a lifeline. She loved him, but he was wrong. "I'll never forget you," she whispered. "Tell Nate I…I said goodbye." She pulled away and hurried out the back of the café, feeling more miserable than ever before. Her world had just come to an end.

* * *

During the next week, Nate went through the motions. He concentrated on his job, but that was about all. He didn't want to eat and trying to sleep was hell. He spent most of his free time in his workshop, trying anything to keep from thinking about Tori.

When she crept into his head, he'd wonder what he could have done differently to make her stay. But it finally came down to the fact she didn't care about him. The sooner he faced that, the faster he could move on.

As if things weren't bad enough, he'd received another blow. The bank loan wasn't enough to cover the inflated price he'd been forced to pay for the Double H.

He had to tell the family.

After his shift, he drove home, but instead of going to his apartment, he walked to his mother's back door. Inside, he found her at the stove cooking, while Shane and Emily set the table. Guess this was as good a time as any to break the bad news.

"The bank can't give me the full amount of the loan I need for the ranch."

"Oh, Nate," his mother gasped. "That's awful. Don't worry, I have some money saved. And I can borrow from my retirement."

"No! Mom, I'd never let you do that."

Shane spoke up. "Nate, you put up a lot of money for my business. If I had it to give back to you I would, but everything I have is tied up."

"No, Shane. When I loaned you that money, I told

you not to pay me back until you showed a profit. I meant it."

Nate sighed in frustration. He'd been so close. "This was all a shot in the dark, anyway. I mean, it would have taken me years to get the ranch back in shape. Not to mention the cost."

"You can't give up, Son," Betty said just as the phone rang. She reached for it. "Hello." She listened to the caller. "Yes, I know who you are." She smiled. "Yes, he's right here." She held out the phone to Nate. "It's Audrey Brighton from the Seaside Gallery."

Nate frowned as he took the receiver. He didn't know anyone named Audrey. "This is Sheriff Hunter."

"I'm actually looking for Nate Hunter, the wood carver."

"I guess that's me, too."

"Well, it's an honor to talk with you, Nate. I'm Audrey Brighton. I have six of your carved figurines here in my gallery. Your work is exquisite, and I hope you'll allow me to sell five of the carvings."

"I have no idea what you're talking about. What carvings?"

His mother spoke up. "They're mine," she told him.

"Audrey, can you hold a moment?" Nate asked, and then placed a hand over the mouthpiece. "Okay, Mom, talk fast."

Betty straightened, refusing to be intimidated. "Audrey is a friend of Tori's," she began. "She runs a gallery in Monterey, California, and she agreed to look at your work. So Tori and I sent her a few of the figurines you made for me."

"Tori went behind my back?"

"No. Tori wanted to tell you, but I decided you'd get all grumpy and irritated. Just like you are now." Her eyes widened. "You have a chance now, Son. Don't blow it. This art dealer wants to sell those carvings."

Nate had to slow down his excitement. "But I made them for you."

Betty smiled fondly. "And I treasured them. I kept the ones from when you were younger. But Audrey is offering you money—money you need right now for the Double H." She touched his hand. "Wouldn't it be wonderful to tell your grandkids how you saved their heritage? Sell them, Son."

Nate had trouble believing any of this as he put the phone to his ear. "Ms. Brighton. They belong to my mother…she says you may sell them."

"Wonderful," she gasped. "I'll send you a contract. Also, I know it's short notice, Nate, but I'm having a new-artist showing this next weekend and I'd like to feature more of your work. I need eight to ten more pieces, but I'll take anything you have."

Nate's head was reeling. In the week since Tori had left, he'd been carving every night. But he'd only finished two pieces and started on another. "I don't have that many."

His mother took the phone from him. "Audrey, he'll have those carvings to you before the weekend. And yes, go ahead and overnight the contract for the other figurines. Thank you so much. Goodbye."

"Mom, what are you doing? I just said, I don't have enough for a showing."

"Oh, yes, you do. You've given dozens of your carvings away as gifts over the years," she said as she dialed the phone. "There isn't a person in this town that wouldn't be willing to help you, Nathan Edward Hunter. It's time you thought of yourself for a change."

Just then Emily returned to the kitchen carrying two figurines. "You can have these, Nate." She placed her carved horses on the table.

These were two of his favorite pieces. He smiled, remembering he'd spent hours working on them. "Oh, Em, I gave you…" He swallowed hard. "You love these."

"I love you more." She hugged him. "Please, Nate, for once will you let us help *you?* You need the money for the ranch. A ranch that belongs to our family. You want to get back part of our heritage. I'm a Hunter, too, and I want to do my part."

"So do I," Shane said. "The mountain lion you gave me for my sixteenth birthday is displayed in my office. Take it."

His mother spoke into the receiver. "Sam. We need your help. It's for Nate."

Nate couldn't talk from the ache in his chest. He'd spent years trying to do what his father would want, to help his family. But maybe this one time, it was okay to take something for himself.

It was just that without Tori his heart wasn't in it.

* * *

Four days later, Nate received a check for a generous amount from the sale of his mother's carvings. He put the money toward the down payment on the ranch, and made arrangements with the loan officer to wait another two weeks for the rest.

He'd just sent off ten more carved figurines to the Seaside Gallery in Monterey. He couldn't believe the friends and teachers who'd returned their carvings so he could have a show.

A little after noon, Nate walked into the café and automatically looked for Tori. Old habits were hard to break. He had to face facts—he wasn't going to see her again. She was back in San Francisco getting on with her life. The sooner he got that through his head the better off he'd be.

"Nate," Sam called as he came out of the kitchen. "You here for lunch?"

"Sure. It's quiet today." Nate accepted a glass of iced tea and sat down at the counter when he spotted Heather. "How's your new waitress working out?"

"She's eager. But Tori can never be replaced."

Nate didn't want to hear about Tori. He'd finally managed to get through a night without dreaming about holding her in his arms…kissing her…loving her. "Yeah, but we all knew she was only here temporarily."

Sam stood at the counter. "You ever wonder why she took off so fast?"

"No, and it's no longer my concern."

Before Sam could speak, the bell sounded over the

door and Ernie walked in. "Nate, good, you're here. I have a problem." He sat down on the next stool. "It's Tori's Corvette. What should I do about it?"

"She didn't pay you?"

"Yeah, she paid in full a week ago. Not that I don't love that car, but you'd think that she'd have taken it with her." Ernie pushed back his baseball cap and scratched his head. "Isn't that the damnedest thing, Sam? Tori paid for the repairs, but she left her car here."

Sam looked at Nate. "Yeah, it's the damnedest thing."

Just then Betty came through the glass door carrying a small package. "This was sent to the house. It's from the gallery, so I thought it might be important."

Nate took the box, used his knife to cut away the tape and opened it. Inside, he removed the bubble wrap and found the carved angel. His heart began to pound. Tori's angel. There was a note.

Nate,
I'm sending this back to you, so you can return it to Tori. She refused to let me sell it, even though I had numerous customers who would pay dearly for this special piece. I have a feeling this angel is one of a kind, just like Tori.
                                Sincerely, Audrey

"Oh, Nate. Tori loved this carving." His mother looked at him and whispered, "I can't understand why she left…" She stopped and blinked rapidly. "I've got to get back to school." Betty headed for the door.

"And I've got to get back to the shop," Ernie said. "Nate, let me know about the car."

That left Sam at the counter. "Well, aren't you going to add your two cents?" Nate asked.

"If you'd just think back, you'd realize that everything Tori did was because she wanted you to be happy."

He wouldn't let himself hope. "Then why did she leave me?"

Sam folded his arms. "Because it was the only way you could get the ranch. I'd bet anything it was her father bidding against you. The day of the auction, I was standing in the back of the crowd and saw her talking with him. She didn't look happy. Then I noticed there was some kind of exchange between Sheridan and that guy bidding against you. Then Tori grabbed at her father's hand and began pleading with him."

"And you know this for sure?"

"Tori didn't deny it when I asked her about it. She was practically crying when she said to tell you goodbye. Then she just ran out of here." Sam sighed. "And now it looks like at least you got the Double H."

"I want Tori more than the damn ranch," Nate muttered, not realizing he'd spoken the words out loud.

"Did you tell her that?"

"She didn't give me a chance." He suddenly remembered that she'd said she only planned to return to San Francisco for six months. She'd wanted to come back to

Haven. He'd never asked her to, just accused her of wanting her father to chase after her. Nate looked at Sam.

"You said her father had something to do with driving up the bid."

Sam nodded. "I'd bet the café on it. That mystery buyer suddenly lost interest after Tori went to talk to Sheridan."

"How can you be sure?"

"Let's find out." Sam grabbed the phone and dialed information. "I was curious so I talked to Charlie Shaw after the auction. He showed me the bidder's business card. He's Trent Knox from a company called Sherco in San Francisco, California. That's too close to a coincidence." The operator came on the line. "Yes, I need the number of Sherco Corporation in San Francisco. And please connect me." Sam waited, and when the receptionist answered, he asked for Trent Knox. He waited and finally nodded. "No, thank you. I'll just try back later." Sam hung up. "See, the man works there, Nate. It could be another Trent Knox, but that's too much of a coincidence for me."

Nate felt his anger growing. "So her father used her friendship with me to blackmail her into going home."

"No, Nate, Sheridan used Tori's *love* for you."

Nate felt worse because he could have helped her. "She asked me for six months, but I thought it was just an excuse to let me down easy. God, she must hate me."

"I doubt it, but why don't you find out?" Sam suggested. "Ernie said her car is paid up. Didn't she promise you some driving time for all you did for her? I think a road trip to the West Coast would pretty much fulfill that promise."

Nate's excitement started to fade. "How can I ask her to give up her life in San Francisco to live on a run-down ranch?"

Sam cocked an eyebrow. "Give her a chance, son. You might be surprised what she chooses. I know for a fact that she's always wanted a home, a family. If I'm not mistaken, you can offer her both things."

Nate wanted to believe. He loved Tori and hoped she would give him one more chance. He grabbed the angel and headed out the door, knowing he needed all the help he could get to bring his Tori home.

Tori glanced out the window of her new executive office. It was cold and damp today, just like her mood. She glanced over her shoulder and saw the stack of work on her desk, but couldn't seem to gather any enthusiasm for doing her job. Not that her father had bugged her about her slow progress. In fact, he'd given her a pretty wide berth since her return. Maybe the man had changed.

No, not J. C. Sheridan. He hadn't changed, but she had. And after her five weeks in Haven, she'd found she would never be satisfied here. For the first time, she'd found someone who made her happy. Nate Hunter. But once again she'd let her father's threats take it all away.

She'd had a man who cared for her, one she cared

about. He'd offered her everything she'd ever dreamed about, the chance to have a home, a family.

Okay, she had stopped her father's bidding on the Double H, but she should have told Nate the truth. Instead, she'd let him think that she wanted her old life back. Well, she hated her old life.

Tori drew a long breath and released it. It was time to renegotiate with J.C. She walked out of her office and paused at her assistant's desk. "Call my father and tell him I'm on my way to see him," she said, and took off down the hall toward the president's office.

Tori was shaking, but that didn't slow her gait. No way could she back down now, not when her happiness was at stake. Without knocking, she opened the door. J. C. Sheridan was seated behind his massive desk.

He glanced at her. "Victoria, this really isn't a good time."

She shut the door. "This will take only thirty seconds." She marched across the plush carpet and stood before him. "How many shares of my stock do you need for controlling interest in Sherco?"

That got the man's attention and he stopped reading. "About two-thirds of your shares."

"You've got it. But I want out of Sherco. Now."

J.C. studied her for a moment, then finally nodded. Without another word, she swung around and walked out. Excitement raced through her; she felt a smile spread across her face as she headed back to her office. She was free. Free to go and do what she wanted.

The first place she was headed was Haven. She needed to get her car, and she hoped Nate would ask her to stay.

Back in her office, she phoned her lawyer to start the stock transfer. After she hung up she noticed the box on her desk. She immediately opened the package to find her angel.

She picked it up and cradled it against her chest. "Oh, Nate, please don't give up on me," she whispered.

A familiar voice said, "I was going to ask you the same thing."

Tori's gaze darted to the door where Nate stood. Dressed in new creased jeans, black boots and a rich blue, starched Western shirt, he took her breath away.

"Nate… How did you get past security?"

He held up his sheriff's badge. "I told your secretary I needed to return something to you. Your angel." He walked into the room and closed the door. "I was told by a friend of yours that you never wanted to part with her."

She swallowed. "Audrey?"

Nate's heart pounded as he made his way around the desk. "She's my friend, too. In fact, she's going to handle my work exclusively. Tori, how can I thank you for sending her my carvings?"

Nate was really here. "There's no reason to thank me. Your talent is too good not to be noticed."

"Mom said the same thing, but I was too stubborn to listen," he said. "Thank you. The money I've made from the figurines will help me move faster with the improvements on the Double H."

She forced a smile and placed her figurine on her desk. He was just here to thank her. "I'm happy for you, Nate. You've gotten everything you've wanted."

"Not everything, Tori." Nate grasped her hand and was happy when she didn't resist. "I've been stubborn about a lot of other things, too." He took a breath and his gaze roamed over her beautiful face. He fought the desire to pull her into his arms. "I was stubborn when I let you walk away. I knew you had a career before you came to Haven and how important you are to this company. But you're important to me, too. And if you need six months, I want you to take it. Take all the time you need. I just want you to know that I'll be waiting for you. You are more important to me that the Double H. If you want to live here, then I'll move to San Francisco." He squeezed her hands. "I love you, Tori Sheridan," he breathed. "I know I have no right to say that, not after the way I treated you—"

He watched as tears flooded her eyes. "God, Tori. I'm sorry. Please, just don't cry."

"I can't help it," she whispered. "Oh, Nate. I don't need time, I've already resigned and I was coming to Haven, to you. I love you—"

Nate's mouth covered hers, smothering the last of her words. He didn't need to hear any more. He needed to feel her in his arms, pressed against him. The touch and taste of her was like heaven. He finally released her, but only because they both needed air.

"Tori, I know what you did for me to keep your father from buying the ranch. I wish I'd known that day." He brought her hand to his lips and kissed it. "I care more about you than any piece of land."

Tori took a breath. "No, Nate. The Double H Ranch belongs to the Hunters. My father was only using it as a way to get me back here. But don't worry. He'll never come between us again. I just signed over the controlling shares of Sherco stock to him. J.C. has what he wants."

Nate frowned. "Tori, I never wanted you to give away your heritage just só I can have mine."

"Sherco was never my heritage. This company is my father's baby." She slipped her arms around his neck, loving the feel of his strength and his gentleness, and the love she saw mirrored in his eyes. "If you're worried I'll be broke, don't be. I'm still on the boards of my maternal grandfather Foster's businesses."

"Businesses?"

She nodded. "Two manufacturing plants in the East, an oil field in Texas and a horse-breeding farm in southern California."

He whistled. "How did I ever think you'd be happy to get a room over a diner?"

"Oh, but I was, Nate. I was truly happy for the first time in my life. I loved living in Haven. I had friends—Sam, Shane, Emily and your mother. You're the kindest man I've ever known. You didn't care about me because of who I was. You cared about me for me. Please don't tell me that my having money changes how you feel about me."

"Oh, darlin', nothing could change that." He frowned. "But are you sure you want to marry a poor rancher from Arizona?"

Tori's heart stopped, then began to race. Was he making all her dreams come true? "You're far from poor, Nate. Besides, I don't remember being asked to marry anybody."

She watched as he swallowed. He was just as nervous as she was. He lowered his head and kissed her sweetly, then reached into his jeans pocket and pulled out a ring.

She stared at the antique diamond ring through watery eyes. "Nate…" she breathed.

"This was my grandmother's ring." He released a long breath and went down on one knee. "I'd planned to do this in a special place I'd picked out, but wherever we're together is special. I love you so much, Tori. I want to share a life with you. I want you to have my children and together we can raise them on Hunter land. I want us to grow old together. Will you marry me?"

"Oh, Nate. Yes, I'll marry you."

She held out her hand and he slipped the ring on her finger. He stood, drew her into his arms and kissed her soundly.

With a groan he released her. "I hope you don't want a long engagement."

"How fast can you get the ranch house livable?"

"Shane promised he could finish it in less than a month. He's been working on the place nights and weekends."

Tori placed her head against his chest, feeling the pounding of his heart. "You're an eager bridegroom."

"You've made me eager since I found you sleeping in your car."

"I believe you were lusting over my Corvette."

Nate reached into his other pocket and pulled out the set of keys. "Let's just say you were both quite a package." He'd never realized he could feel this way about anyone, never thought that he'd find a woman like Tori.

Her eyes widened. "You drove my car here?"

"If I'm not mistaken, Ms. Sheridan, I had accumulated a lot of driving time." He placed a soft kiss on her lips, his teeth tugging on her lower lip. She couldn't help whimpering. "And I hope to rack up a lot more."

"How much time do you have before we have to go back?"

"Six days. But if it took longer to convince you to marry me, I was willing to sacrifice my job."

"I think a week is enough time to show you around town." She raised up on her toes and kissed him so thoroughly, she felt light-headed.

"But first, I think we should start at my place for some serious negotiations about our future."

"I like the way you think." He kissed her again. Tori just clung to him, her love for this man burst from every part of her being. Thanks to fate, she'd found a special man.

She'd also finally found what she'd been looking for. Love and family.

Epilogue

Tori Hunter stood on the back porch at the Double H Ranch. She hugged her sweater to her body to ward off the February chill as she looked out over the glorious landscape of her new home.

She and Nate had been married six months ago right here on Hunter land. They'd chosen the original homestead for the ceremony. She'd wanted Nate to know that she truly felt a part of his dream for the Double H. After a short honeymoon in Maui, they'd come back to the ranch house, completely restored by Hunter Construction. She'd decorated her new home with her mother's antiques that had been in storage. They fit in the Double H perfectly, just as Tori did. Every morning she woke up next to Nate, still hardly believing this was her life and that this was her man who loved her and that they were building a future together.

Tori looked to the barn as Nate walked out of his new workshop, where he'd spent his days off carving his much-in-demand figurines. After his successful show, Audrey wanted a one-man show next fall.

After talking with the two hired ranch hands, Nate tossed Tori a sexy grin, then he started for the house. Although he was still Sheriff Nate Hunter—until the end of his term—and a talented wood carver—he was really a rancher in his heart. And although she was the new grade-five teacher at Haven Elementary, she was trying her best to be a rancher's wife.

Nate climbed to the porch and pulled her into his arms. "Good morning, Mrs. Hunter." He kissed her thoroughly. The familiar jolt of awareness brought back memories of the way she and Nate had made love just hours ago.

"Good morning to you, too. Why didn't you wake me?"

"Because I wouldn't have wanted to leave the bed. And I thought you needed the sleep."

"Thank you." She nodded toward his workshop. "Did you get any work done?"

"Some." He nipped at her mouth. "But I was distracted by the thought of you." He hugged her tighter. "I wanted to climb back in bed with you."

She would have welcomed him with open arms. "But you need to get ready for your show."

"I want to spend time with you." He cocked an eyebrow. "Are you sure we're not taking on too much?"

She smiled. He didn't know the half of it. "Speaking of doing too much, remember when we talked about a family?"

Before her husband could answer, the foreman called to him. Nate gave some instructions, then turned back to her. "What were you saying?"

His silver gaze bored into hers and suddenly she felt shy. "It's just that… I know we talked about waiting…"

He laughed. "Waiting? Since when have we ever waited? Do you realize that six months ago, I'd only just met you?" He kissed the end of her nose. "And I fell in love with you in an instant."

"Well, with your new career as an artist, and getting this ranch back…we are pretty busy." She raised a hand against his solid chest. Her Nate was a handsome man. No wonder she couldn't resist him. "I mean, you need time to work on your carvings, and I'd planned to teach for at least another year…"

Nate frowned. What was Tori trying to say? Was all this too much for her? He knew he was spread pretty thin and hadn't spent as much time with her as he wanted.

"Maybe we should have waited to start the herd. If it's too much—"

"No, Nate. We both wanted to rebuild the ranch. But something's come up that we didn't expect…"

Nate started to speak when he saw his brother's truck barreling toward the house. It finally skidded to a stop and Shane jumped out.

"Wonder what's gotten into him?" Nate released her as his brother came up the steps. "Hey, you're out early."

"Then maybe you can give me a job as a ranch hand because I'm out of the construction business."

"Hold on just a minute. What's happened?"

"Kurt Easton is the problem. I knew I should have never gotten involved with him in this housing development. He's always been out to get the Hunters."

Nate wasn't a fan of Easton, either. "What did he do?"

"He's convinced his partners to bring in a project manager. Hell, he's basically saying I can't do my job."

Just then another car pulled up, and Betty, Sam and Emily climbed out. Suddenly there was a crowd on the porch. There were kisses all round, then they all trooped into the kitchen.

"I still can't get over this place," Betty said as she set a covered casserole dish on the granite counter. "It's absolutely beautiful."

"I love it, too," Tori said as she started a fresh pot of coffee, then took a pitcher of orange juice out of the refrigerator. "Can I fix anyone some breakfast? I have plenty of bacon and eggs."

Nate watched Tori's color suddenly fade. She put the pitcher on the table. "Excuse me." She shot out of the kitchen to the bathroom off the hall and slammed the door. A faint retching sound was heard even through the thick walls.

Panicked, Nate turned to his mother and saw her smile.

"Looks like I'm going to be a grandmother."

Nate managed to swallow as he glanced from one grinning face to another. Tori was pregnant? He looked at his mother again. "Are you sure?"

"Maybe you should ask your wife," Betty said as she gave him a nudge down the hall.

Lying on the bathroom rug, Tori was too miserable to be embarrassed. Well, now she didn't need to find the right way to tell her husband about the baby. She heard the soft knock on the door, then Nate stepped inside.

A tear found its way down her cheek. "I was going to tell you. I know we wanted to wait…"

He sat down beside her and brushed his fingers through her hair. "When did you find out?"

She sat up slowly. "I suspected last week, then this morning I took a pregnancy test." With his help she stood, washed off her face and brushed her teeth.

Nate leaned against the sink and drew her between his legs. "A baby. Oh, God, Tori, I've dreamed of you carrying my child."

Her eyes searched his. "You sure? You aren't just saying that?"

He slipped his arms around her. "No, I just said I'd like to wait because I knew how badly you wanted to teach."

"I want a baby, too. Your baby. But the ranch—and your career."

He shook his head. "You and this child are more important than any career." His voice was suddenly husky. "I love you so much."

"I love you, too." She hugged him.

His chest rumbled with laughter. "You said you wanted a family. You've got a husband, a mother, a brother and a sister. Now, you'll have a baby, too. Do you think this is a good beginning?"

Tori looked up and kissed the man who'd given her everything, especially his love. "I think it's perfect."

* * * * *

And don't miss
the next compelling episode
of Patricia Thayer's new miniseries:
LOVE AT THE GOOD TIME CAFÉ
FAMILIAR ADVERSARIES
(Silhouette Romance #1779)
by Patricia Thayer

The Hunter and Easton families had been feuding for
the past sixty years. And lately, fortune had been shin-
ing on the Hunters. That was, until a feisty European
beauty got set to dish out a delicious payback. It
seems the impetuous redhead has been named boss to
the same Hunter playboy who once broke her heart....

Take a sneak peek at
FAMILIAR ADVERSARIES
by Patricia Thayer
Silhouette Romance #1779
Coming August 2005

Chapter One

If this wasn't the worst day of his life it was damn close.

Early Monday morning, Shane Hunter turned off the highway onto the dirt-and-gravel road. Immediately the old truck's lack of suspension had him bouncing in the seat. He eased his foot off the gas and steered to avoid the potholes. He released a breath as he glanced at the billboard sign that read Paradise Estates in bold letters. In the corner, in smaller type, were the words Hunter Construction. He couldn't help but feel pride. Barely two years ago he'd started the company, and now he was building the first phase of Haven, Arizona's, newest housing development. Thirty-five single-family homes. Every dime he had or could borrow was wrapped up in this project. And if luck and the weather held, Hunter Construction was on its way.

His life would be nearly perfect if only he didn't have to work for Kurt Easton. There wasn't a resident of Haven who hadn't heard about the Easton family's ongoing feud with the Hunters. From the start Easton had done everything he could to push Shane off the project, especially after there had been two break-ins at the site. Not much damage was done the first time, but in the second incident several pieces of valuable equipment had been stolen. Shane had hired more security, but Easton wasn't satisfied. He'd persuaded investors to hire a project manager to keep the project on schedule and to keep an eye on Shane.

Shane drove past the first row of the framed two-story structures. Farther down were several stacks of lumber and building supplies behind a chain-link fence. He continued on to the construction trailer where he spotted his crew standing around outside. Shane checked his watch. It was after 7:00 a.m. What was going on? His crew knew their jobs. He'd given the supervisor the list of assignments last Friday. He parked his truck, climbed out and went straight to the framing foreman, Rod Hendon.

"Rod, why is everyone standing around?"

The foreman shook his head. "It's not my call, Shane. The project manager said to wait until you got here."

Shane's stomach knotted and he had to fight to keep his cool. Easton would love to see him blow up over this. "Where is this project manager?"

Rod pointed at the trailer. "Inside. And I'll tell you right now, you aren't going to like what you find."

Shane didn't doubt it, but over the weekend his brother, Nate, had convinced him that he'd need to keep a cool head if he wanted to complete this job. Shane marched off toward the trailer. Fine, he'd work with a manager, but first, they needed to get a few things straight and the sooner the better.

Shane climbed the wooden steps, pulled open the door, and stepped inside. "What the hell gives you the right to keep my crew from starting work?" He froze when he found a woman, not a man, sitting behind his desk.

She was an auburn-haired beauty with pale creamy skin, and a wide inviting mouth with full kissable lips. And when she looked up at him with those large green eyes he could only find enough air in his lungs to breathe out her name. "Mariah…"

"Hello, Shane," she said in that soft husky voice he hadn't been able to get out of his head for the past dozen years. "It's been a long time."

Not long enough to forget. He watched as she came around the desk. At five-eight, Mariah Easton's body was absolute perfection. She filled out a pair of faded jeans nicely. Too nicely. She wore an oversize chambray shirt that showed off her delicate frame, but also hid the generous curve of her breasts. But he knew they were full and lush. Whoa. Don't go heading down memory lane. You'll only get in trouble. He shook his head and returned to the present.

"If you're waiting for your father, he isn't here."

Mariah shook her head, causing her wild mane to

move against her shoulders. "I've already talked with Dad this morning. He would have been here but I told him I wanted to handle this on my own."

He didn't like the sound of this. "Handle what?"

"I'm the new project manager."

This was the worst day of his life. "The hell you say."